SAVAGE PRINCE

Book One of the Savage Trilogy

MEGHAN

MARCH

ISBN: 978-1-943796-15-1

Editor: Pam Berehulke
Bulletproof Editing
www.bulletproofediting.com

Cover design: @ Letitia Hassar
R.B.A. Designs
www.rbadesigns.com

Cover photo: @ Weston Carls
www.westoncarls.com

Visit my website at www.meghanmarch.com.

ABOUT THIS BOOK

Who knew things could get even darker and dirtier in New Orleans? *New York Times* bestselling author Meghan March introduces the Savage Prince of the city, the man you never want to meet.

I do what I want and who I want. I don't follow anyone's rules—even my own.

I knew I shouldn't touch her, but it didn't stop me. Didn't stop me the second time either. Only made me want a third.

My lifestyle suits the savage I am, and she doesn't.

But Temperance Ransom is my newest addiction, and I'm nowhere near ready to quit her yet.

I'll have her my way, even if it means dragging her into the darkness.

Hopefully, it doesn't kill us both.

Savage Prince is the first book of the Savage Trilogy, set in the same world as *Ruthless King*; however, you do not need to read the Mount Trilogy to devour this scandalously hot story.

SAVAGE PRINCE

CHAPTER 1

Temperance

WHY IS HE WEARING A MASK?

Instinctively, I take a step back as the heavy door swings open, revealing the rest of the doorman's tall body and the other half of the ornate red-and-black leather mask obscuring his face.

It's not Mardi Gras season anymore, and this antebellum mansion is dozens of miles away from Bourbon Street, where spirits are high and revelry is in full swing, no matter the time of year.

Louisiana, you're beautiful, but you're also creepy as hell at night sometimes.

The doorman gestures for me to enter, and I hesitate on the threshold for one final beat, clutching my bag to my side before stepping through the archway. He closes the massive wooden door behind me with a decisive thud and throws a long bolt.

I'm locked in. *What did I get myself into?*

Chills skate over my skin, and my blazer does little to stop the shiver working through me.

This is not a haunted house. Or a dungeon. It's a potential customer. I tell my overactive imagination to calm down but blood pounds in my ears, competing with the slow, rhythmic, and visceral beat of the bass coming from somewhere inside.

The sprawling plantation house reminds me of something out of a movie, especially with its massive trees dangling their moss over the banks of the bayou. Mansions and their expensive everything make me more nervous than the gators lurking in that murky water.

My senses shift into high gear as I scan the polished wooden planks of the floor, covered by thick rugs that probably cost more than I make in a year. The muted glow of gaslight sconces adds to the otherworldly feel—at complete odds with the throbbing beat of the club music.

For the dozenth time, I wish I did more research before I showed up for this meeting, but I've been so busy, I can barely manage to shovel three bites of food into my mouth for lunch.

It's worth it, I remind myself. *I have a respectable job now.* There's no mud on the bottom of my shoes to track inside these days.

Even though I know I'm in the right place, my polished designer knock-off pumps itch to beat a path to the door and out to my car . . . except it's not there, because the overly efficient valet drove it away before the front door even opened.

I swallow back a lump of unease but straighten my shoulders and turn my attention to the doorman, who seems to be waiting for me to compose myself.

When I meet his hooded stare, he doesn't speak. I hold out the note that showed up on my desk at Seven Sinners. He takes it from me and glances at the printed text, but still says nothing.

"I'm supposed to meet someone?" I hate that my voice sounds like I'm asking a question rather than making a statement. I shake off the unease and find my assertive tone. "I'm here to meet someone for a business discussion. Can you please direct me to the office?"

The doorman gestures to the opulent staircase before me with the card before offering it back.

My sweaty palms leave smudges on the edges as I snatch it from his grip. I should have known from that fancy cream linen paper that this wouldn't be like the normal bars and clubs I've visited to hawk Seven Sinners Whiskey.

"Thank you." I give him a nod, and once again get zero verbal response. *This place is bizarre.* Time to get in and get out.

Attempting to look unaffected, I stride toward the red-and-gold runner climbing up the stairs.

I'm just here to sell whiskey. All the whiskey.

The treads beneath the soles of my shoes vibrate

more with each step I take. As I round the curve of the staircase, I find another masked man waiting for me at the top.

I offer him my invitation and stare over his shoulder at the light spilling out from beneath a set of closed double doors.

There. That has to be the club. See, nothing different about this place after all.

Except there is, and I don't know if it's my overactive imagination, but I swear I can smell sex in the air. Images of all the things that can possibly be happening behind those doors assail my brain. I force my attention back to the man for direction.

He jerks his head to the side and starts down a wide gold-and-white-striped corridor, away from the doors. He pauses at the corner as though waiting for me to follow him, and I uproot my feet from the floor and stumble forward to catch up with my bag smacking my hip. Instead of leading me farther down the corridor, he steps out of the way to reveal another set of curving stairs and points upward.

Seriously? I thought this was a business meeting, not punishment for missing my date with the gym for the last six months.

My arches cramp in protest as I smooth down my skirt, reset my bag, and climb to the top, but at least this discomfort takes my mind off the peculiar feel of this place.

I'm going to have to sell a ton of whiskey to make

this trip worth it.

When I hit the next landing, there's a third man, this one the size of a linebacker, wearing a matching mask.

Where the hell is everyone else? What kind of club has silent doormen and no tipsy patrons stumbling back and forth to the restroom?

I don't have time to ask either of those questions before masked man number three reads the words on the card I hold out and leads me down a hallway to what I assume must be the manager's office. At least, I hope like hell it is.

An ornate door with an antique brass knob awaits at the end, and he pushes it open and gestures for me to enter with a meaty hand.

I pin my most professional smile on my face and take a deep breath, ready to charm whoever awaits me inside into buying more whiskey than they plan.

With a confident stride, I make my way inside.

"Hi! I'm Temperance—" I trail off when I realize the chair behind the desk, dimly lit by a simple banker's lamp, is empty.

A quick scan of the rest of the dark room reveals no signs of life.

What the hell?

"Okay, then." I clear my throat, poised to turn around and get the hell out of this place, when a light flickering to life distracts me.

But it's not a light in the office where I've been

shown, but a light in the room next door. A room that I can apparently view through what appears to be a two-way mirror.

Am I really seeing this?

And by this, I mean a monstrous iron-and-wood four-poster bed draped with black silk sheets . . . and restraints.

A bedroom. *A kinky bedroom.*

Holy hell.

I stumble back a step, reaching for the doorknob, but my gaze fixes on the black mask of the woman entering the bedroom and the heavily muscled shirtless man with his palm on the small of her back.

This isn't just any trendy secret club interested in adding top-notch whiskey to their shelves.

It's a *sex club*.

I should be horrified. Running screaming in the opposite direction and out to my car. But instead, I'm rooted to the floor.

I have a front-row seat to one of my dirtiest fantasies. A fantasy I finally got up the nerve to try to fulfill a few months ago, because Lord knows I don't have time to have a relationship, but my search for a non-sketchy sex club in New Orleans fell flat. Google sure as hell didn't have this one on the map, and neither did any of the forums or blog posts I read.

A real underground sex club.

A tingle of excitement, like I've just discovered a secret key to another world, shoots through me as the man shuts the door to their room and slowly circles the woman before pushing her to her knees with one dominant hand on each shoulder. He has the look of a conqueror inspecting his war prize, complete with tribal ink marking his chest and upper arms, and dark leather pants. It's hot as hell.

The rational part of my brain says I should look away, not invade their private scene, but I glance quickly at the door I entered through. No one is bursting in to tell me it's some kind of mistake that I was led here.

The woman, dressed in red lingerie, keeps her gaze downcast, but I'm not nearly as disciplined. I can't take my eyes off her companion as his ass flexes against the leathers.

When he stops in front of her, he releases her shoulder and buries one hand in her honey-blond hair, gripping her at the base of her neck, forcing her attention to his face.

They are completely and utterly absorbed with each other, and neither of them spares even a glance at the wall that serves as my voyeuristic porthole. *Do they know?* They must.

His voice somehow comes loud and clear into this room. "You wanted my attention down there, little girl. You've got it all now."

My heart thumps harder as he reaches for the flap of his leathers with his other hand and yanks it open, freeing his heavy cock.

I bite down on my lower lip to stifle the hushed *oh my God* dying to break free. The sting from my teeth serves as a reminder that this isn't one of my dreams.

This is real.

My conscience wars with me, telling me to turn away. Go back down the stairs. Run out the front door. Find my car and get the hell out of here.

But that and any other thought of business dies away as he wraps one palm around his thick cock and gives it a rough tug before thumbing the tip. The ruddy reddish-purple shaft seems to pulse against his grip, and my lip trembles as my thighs clench.

Why is it so frigging hot to see a man handle himself like that?

Using his grip on her hair, he guides her lips toward the head.

Sweet Lord. I shouldn't be turned on by this. But my sweaty palms and the thumping pulse that has taken up residence between my legs expose my lie.

This is the hottest thing I've ever seen in person.

"You want this? Is that why you've been acting like a little brat?" His words are muted, like the sound is being piped into the office through speakers, or maybe it's because the blood roaring through my head is drowning out normal sound. Either way, his gruff, deep voice drags over my senses, making goose bumps rise across my skin.

"Yes, sir." The woman's chin bounces as she licks

her lips.

He drags her face an inch closer to his cock. "Show me how much."

My nipples pebble against my bra at his rough order. Heat, completely inappropriate fiery heat, streaks through me as one of the woman's hands dives between her legs.

"You don't get to touch yourself until I tell you to. I'll turn that ass of yours red before you finger that wet little cunt."

I squeeze my thighs together like he's somehow threatening me. Ordering me. Dominating me.

And I wish he were.

"I want your hands on my legs. I'm going to fuck your face. Remind you who owns these lips."

A quiet moan echoes through the room, and I'm ninety-nine percent sure it came from her and not me. Okay, ninety percent sure.

I squirm, my chest rising and falling faster as she rests her palms on his muscled thighs and he feeds his cock into her mouth inch by inch.

Oh my God. I can't watch. I shouldn't watch. I'm not a dirty little thing who likes to watch. I'm not. Really. I'm not.

But I'm a filthy liar, because none of the words I use to berate myself make me tear my gaze away from the most erotic scene I've ever seen play out.

He shifts his grip, using one hand to cup her chin and tilt her head to the angle of his liking as he powers deeper inside, more of his rock-hard shaft disappearing with each thrust.

His growl echoes through the room, and I can feel it in the wet heat between my legs like a heartbeat.

"You feel that? You want more?"

Her plaintive, muffled cry for *more* unleashes another round of shivers as my breathing shallows. My inner muscles clench as I imagine a cock sliding past my lips and down my throat. My gag reflex flutters at the all-too-real and intense feeling.

That could be me.

Her fingertips curl around his legs and mine do the same, but instead of smooth skin, mine scrape across the fabric of my skirt. Two thin layers. That's all that separates me from making myself come in approximately 2.5 seconds.

My fingers tense, stretching as though itching to move.

Don't you even think about it, Temperance. Don't you dare think about it.

But then he slows his movements, pulling his cock from between her lips. It glistens in the dim light as he wraps a hand around it and strokes. The woman's need is visible in every tense muscle of her body as she fixates on his lazy movements.

"I'm not coming in that pretty mouth. Not tonight. Tonight, I'm taking that ass you've been teasing me with. Bending you over so I can see your cunt and your tight little hole. I get so fucking hard when I think about turning it red before I finally bury myself inside."

Oh, for fuck's sake. This isn't even fair.

I swallow the saliva filling my mouth and back up until I bump into the edge of a desk. My heels wobble, and I reach out a hand to steady myself.

I cross my legs and shift back and forth to try to stave off the urge to do more. *I'm here for business. Not for pleasure.* But the reminder is a fleeting one, disappearing from my brain as soon as he speaks again.

"Tell me you want me to take your ass. Own it. Make it mine so you never forget who you belong to."

The woman's mouth drops open and her tongue darts out to wet the corner. "Yes, sir."

He reaches down and extends a hand. "Stand."

She complies by sliding her fingers into his and rising gracefully to her feet. Then his movement turns rougher as he spins her around and bends her over the end of the bed.

My heart thunders as I squeeze my thighs together, and the man yanks the crotch of her thong aside, baring her pussy and ass.

It's obscene, but I can't look away.

My fingernails dig into my leg through my skirt as he barks another order.

"Spread your legs."

The uncompromising tone of his voice ricochets through my body, and part of me wants to comply like the woman as she slides her legs a few inches farther apart, creating an even more indecent visual.

The heat between my legs jumps what feels like a million degrees, and I suddenly wish I'd done laundry this week, because then I'd be wearing underwear. Instead, wetness gathers and threatens to drip down my inner thighs.

A dirty, shameful feeling curls inside me and I squirm, squeezing my legs even tighter together, but it doesn't change the way my body responds. Especially not when he claps his palm between her legs with a smack. Her hips jerk and a moan spills out from between her lips.

Oh good Lord. He spanked her pussy.

I cover my mouth with one hand to silence my own sharp breath, and my teeth dig into my skin.

He plunges a finger inside, moving it out and then back in. "This is mine. You flash it at anyone else, and I'll tie you up and drag you to the edge so many times, you'll be delirious before I ever let you come. That's a fucking promise."

He pulls free of her body and lands a hard smack on her ass. She screeches as his handprint blooms red on her skin before he covers it with a firm grip, and the sound coming from her mouth turns into a moan.

"Please."

"You know I love to hear you beg." He releases her and lands another blow. "But you'll remember your manners or get nothing."

"Please, sir!"

Her wail wraps around me as he caresses the cheek he just stung. The desk bites into my ass, but I know it's not the same.

I want to know what that feels like.

The truth blows through my mind like a hurricane. Unstoppable. Unashamed. Un-fucking-believable.

Is it possible to spontaneously orgasm? I have to get out of here. But my fingers curl around the sharp edge of the wood as though it's the only thing keeping me grounded.

"Beg me."

With my nipples harder than diamonds, I wait for her to beg. *Please. I want to see—*

She does.

Oh good Lord, I'm going to hell.

He grips his cock with one hand, her ass with the other, and lines up the head with her entrance. "Pussy first. You're not ready for me yet."

The pace of my breathing nears hyperventilation.

I need to do something. I have to—

Any capacity for rational thought is ripped from my brain as he buries his cock inside her and her scream fills my ears. He pounds into her over and over, and I hate her. I hate that she's receiving his perfectly rough thrusts that rip moans of ecstasy from her throat, and all I have is the clenching emptiness between my legs.

I want that. I need that. It's been way too long since I felt . . . anything *like this.* Actually, I've never felt anything remotely like this.

This dark edge of pleasure is something I've only read about. Wished for. Dreamed about.

Her moans and cries intensify, and he praises her. I close my eyes, letting his words wash over me, and pretend he's whispering them to me.

My fingers edge toward the hem of my skirt and I draw it up inch by inch. *I need more. Just a little—*

"My naughty secretary should know better than to touch herself during work hours."

The deep, rasping words come out of the shadows and brush over my skin, leaving goose bumps in their wake.

Shock freezes my movements, my fingertips locked on the material of my skirt, as a chair creaks and the disembodied voice takes the shape of a tall, broad-shouldered man stepping into the dim pool of light. A black leather mask obscures the top half of his face, but his piercing blue eyes burn hotter than a five-alarm fire. They sear my skin everywhere they touch.

"Do you have anything to say for yourself, Ms. Smith?" His sculpted lips are perfect—except for the fact they called me by the wrong name.

"Umm, uhh . . ." I stammer as I attempt to find words that can possibly apply to this insane situation. "I-I'm sorry, I think you have the wrong—"

His eyes narrow, but the heat remains intact. "Nobody argues with me in my office. Strike two, Ms. Smith."

"But I'm here for—" I make another attempt to explain his mistake, but he cuts me off with a tilt of his head.

"Whatever I want." He emphasizes each word as he takes another step toward me. "And tonight, what I want is *you*."

My teeth dig into my bottom lip as he slides his suit jacket off his shoulder and down one arm before repeating the motion with the other. His movements reveal a crisp white shirt perfectly tailored to broad shoulders, thick biceps, and a narrow waist.

Holy wow. He's sex in a suit.

"If you're still in this office in ten seconds, I'll take that to mean *yes, sir, I'm ready.*"

I glance at the door and back at him as he begins the countdown.

"Ten . . ."

CHAPTER 2

Temperance

'M FROZEN STOCK STILL. MY RATIONAL BRAIN IS screaming at me to run for the door, yank it open, and flee while I still can. But the other side of me, the side that searched for a place exactly like this, says I can be anyone he wants me to be tonight, including Ms. Smith.

The only person I *don't* have to be is the utterly boring version of Temperance Ransom I've spent years creating.

"Nine."

His countdown continues as he unfastens a cuff link and folds back the cuff of his white shirt, revealing a muscular forearm covered in colorful ink.

Sweet Lord. Tattoos under a suit? How is that even fair?

"Eight."

My thighs clench involuntarily as he repeats his

calculated movement, revealing more tanned and tattooed skin.

This beautiful man is preparing to discipline his naughty secretary. In a scene. In a sex club.

I should explain his mistake. Really, I should . . . but my pounding pulse argues that I should at least see what else he's hiding under those fancy clothes.

"Seven." He reaches for his tie, loosening the knot before tugging it free. "Six. You're running out of time, *Ms. Smith*."

The extra emphasis on the name seems like a challenge or a test. *Maybe a dare?*

Does he know I'm not her? I'm not wearing a mask, so he can see my face. It has to be obvious . . . unless he's never seen Ms. Smith before and this is a prearranged sexual encounter between strangers. In which case . . .

"Five."

My mouth is no longer the Sahara Desert. No, it's currently experiencing a hundred-year flood as he unfastens the top buttons of his shirt, revealing a perfectly sculpted chest and another piece of delicious artwork. It's the perfect contradiction. With each button, the straight-laced businessman facade falls away to reveal a man I want to devour me.

A man who, from the heat blazing in his eyes, will do a damn good job of it.

"Four."

I need this. His big hands dwarf the buttons but

could easily manhandle me until I'm screaming out my release.

"Three."

Then he parts the sides of his snowy white shirt and reveals washboard abs flanked on either side by tattoos that extend down his ribs to his hips. It's like a frame for a body I didn't know could exist in real life.

This isn't even fair. My gaze skids to a halt when it reaches the sharply cut V and the tattoo that disappears into his suit pants. I bite down on my lip, mostly in an effort to stop the drool. There's no decision to be made here. It's a foregone conclusion. I'm not walking out that door.

"Two."

Is it shallow, basing my choice on his body and how it ripples deliciously as he takes a step toward me? No. It's *primal.* I want him. I don't care that I don't know his name and he doesn't know mine, and we'll never see each other again after tonight.

I need this.

"One." The corner of his lush mouth tugs up on one side, and my nipples and clit pulse in response. "God help you, because now you're fucking *mine.*"

He moves like a panther, quick and efficient, as he reaches out to wrap a hand around both my wrists, capturing them in front of me.

A squeak pops out from between my lips as he tugs me off the desk and spins me around to face it.

He releases me only to press me forward with a hand at my lower back, until my nipples press hard against the wood.

"Do you know what strike three is, Ms. Smith?"

"No," I whisper. *Please tell me it leads to me getting all of him.*

"You didn't wear your mask. How many times am I going to have to spank this peach of an ass to remind you of the rules?"

My mouth drops open to answer, but I have no response.

"For every second you don't answer me, you're adding to your punishment."

My mind races. How many? Do I lie? Tell the truth?

"Three," I say, my voice breathy.

"Three. Plus your hesitation. Plus the fact your ass demands more . . . I say ten."

"But—"

"Go ahead. Argue with me. You might like the outcome." His threats sound like a promise when delivered in that darkly sensual voice.

A cry from the other room steals our attention, and I turn my head to the side to see what's happening. I can't help myself.

"He's fucking her ass, and she loves it."

Shivers dart up my spine, but suddenly the glass of the window frosts, blocking out what's happening in the other room.

"What—" I look over my shoulder, seeking some kind of explanation.

My stranger holds up a small remote that must control the opacity of the glass. "I think you've seen enough. Now it's your turn."

"But—"

Whatever I planned to say next is cut off by the sharp sting of his palm landing on the curve of my ass. Heat radiates when his hand retreats and cold air whooshes before he makes contact with the other side.

Holy crap. It burns with a delicious ribbon of pleasure twining through the tingling. He's not waiting for me to count, so maybe that's not the protocol for this sort of thing. Not that I would know about protocol beyond the books I've read.

I brace for another, but instead he cups my cheeks in his hands and kneads them, intensifying the sensation.

"Fuck. Your ass was made for this."

It takes everything I have not to arch my back and lift up toward him, seeking more contact.

I shouldn't like this so much. Shouldn't want more. Should run away screaming.

But fuck the shoulds and shouldn'ts. Now is the time to *live*. Something I haven't been doing for far too long.

"Done already?" I don't recognize the throaty voice that comes from my lips. I sound bolder and more certain than I have in years.

Instead of raining down blows again, he stills his touch for a moment. "Misguided secretary. If you even knew what I was capable of . . ."

His words trail off as he strokes the curve of my hip with his thumb. He lands four more strikes in quick succession, each landing on untouched areas, extending the delicious burn across my entire ass.

I squirm against the desk, reveling in how good it hurts.

Again, he massages the spots before I count out the remaining strikes in my head. *Four. Three. Two. One.*

Shockingly, I'm not ready for them to end, and my thighs clench together tighter than when I was watching the other couple.

Oh my God. What if someone is watching us?

I attempt to push up off the desk, but his strong hold on my hip keeps me pinned in place.

"If you can't take it—"

"Who's watching us?" The question comes out with a sharp edge, slicing off the remainder of his statement.

His grip tightens on my hip. "No one's watching us."

I should have no reason to believe him. And yet, I do.

The heat of his hard body soaks into my clothes as he leans forward, his heavy chest against my back.

"But I think you would like it if they were." His voice deepens to a rumble, and my entire body tenses.

"No." My reply comes out tentative.

The heat of his breath ghosts over my ear. "You sure about that?" His free hand skates over my skin, this time skimming dangerously close to the juncture of my thighs and the blazing heat of my arousal. "You wouldn't love to have some stranger watching me touch you right now? Knowing that they're wishing they were me? Wishing they had the fucking privilege, but knowing they're out of luck because the only hands touching you tonight are mine?"

His words caress the shell of my ear, but goose bumps rise on every inch of my exposed skin at the images he paints.

"You're a stranger."

He glides a fingertip over the soaked seam of my pussy lips. "Don't think your body cares a whole hell of a lot who I am. Why'd you stay? You could've run. As soon as you realized you were in the wrong place at the wrong time and this scene wasn't set for you— you could've run. But you stayed because you wanted to. Try to deny it."

My stomach drops, and once again, I attempt to rise but he doesn't let me. "I—I . . ." I trail off because I have no excuse for it.

His hand stills. "You can't deny it. Somewhere, hidden in this prim and proper suit is a bad, dirty little thing dying to break free."

He has no idea how right he is. I've kept the chains tight, locking down the wildness from my younger years, all in an effort to break from the mold of my past.

"I should go."

His breath ghosts over my ear again, sending chills down my spine. "Maybe you should, but you won't."

One finger plunges inside my body and my moan fills the silent room.

"That's right, princess. You're mine tonight, and I'm going to take damn good care of you."

Any thoughts of leaving are wiped away as he finger-fucks me with confident strokes until I beg.

"Please. More. I need more."

He grunts, pushing a second finger inside. His two fingers barely fit together, and I press back to feel the stretch.

It has been way, way too long since anyone but me has touched me.

I whimper and moan, losing my iron grip on propriety. Not tonight. Tonight is about getting what I've denied myself for years.

"I need your cock. Now. Please—"

He pulls his fingers free and lands a slap between my thighs, setting off a scream-inducing orgasm.

He spanked my pussy.

I writhe, attempting to move, but he buries a

hand in my hair, keeping me pinned. Maybe it's better that way, because my next instinct is to spin around and fall to my knees in front of him, and find what I hope is a thick cock to go with the rest of him.

"You want my dick? You think you can handle it?"

"Yes!" I scream the answer, and he releases his grip. A few seconds later, I hear the crinkle of foil.

"Might not fit in this tight little pussy. You think you can handle being stuffed full?"

Moisture floods between my legs.

"Big promises—" I start to taunt, but something thick and solid nudges against my soaked entrance.

"Princess, I got big everything." His cocky attitude should be a turnoff, but as he pushes inside, I realize it's not fueled by arrogance, but confidence.

He feels *huge*.

His fingers close around my hair, fisting it at the base of my neck as he continues pushing through my slick channel until he's balls deep.

"Big enough for you?"

"Oh God."

"Hold on to those prayers. Gonna get a little rough."

If I were rational and sane, the word *rough* would have me freaking the hell out, but it doesn't. I reach out and grip the edge of the desk.

"I can take it." My tone is pure challenge, more suited to the rebellious teen of my misspent youth than the professional woman I am today.

It must be the right answer, though, because it unleashes the beast behind me. My stranger draws back before fucking into me with a measured rhythm of deep and then shallow strokes. He relentlessly hits the spots that light my body up. *The man has skills.*

It's the last coherent thought I have as my fingers tighten around the edge of the desk. My head begs to thrash from side to side but is pinned in place by his hand.

He's taking me. Owning me. Dominating me. Leaving me no choice but to take the fucking he's delivering.

And I love it.

Another orgasm builds and threatens to shatter my grip, and when he changes his pattern, my body is thrown into a new level of chaos.

Thrust after thrust, I can't even understand the babbling words spilling from my lips.

I can't stop coming. These aren't multiples . . . they're continuous, and I'm a writhing, moaning body without any coherent thought beyond—*don't stop.*

He doesn't. My control shatters along with my grip.

The blood pounding through my head deafens me, but not enough to miss his roar of ecstasy just before he thrusts slow and shallow.

"Fuck!" He releases my hair to grip both my hips,

pulling them back against him hard as he finally stills.

For long moments, I wait for my heart to burst because it can't handle the beating, but finally, it slows.

This is a moment I'm not prepared for. I don't know what to say. What to do. What to think. How to justify this aberration in my carefully plotted life.

What the hell did I do?

The intensity of the moment fractures as he steps away, the thick length of his cock pulling out of my body. I wait for two long seconds before I flip my skirt down and push off the desk. *I have to get out of here.*

A quick look over my shoulder shows me that his back is turned as he walks toward a door I didn't notice. My logical thoughts are momentarily derailed as my gaze locks on the flex of his perfectly formed ass. *Jesus Christ, how is that fair?*

It doesn't matter. *I have to go. This never should have happened.*

I tear my eyes off his ass, grab my bag, snag my pumps, and bolt for the door barefoot. He doesn't notice my escape until I yank it open.

"What the—" His deep voice cuts off when I slam the door shut behind me and race for the stairs.

Run. Hurry. Hurry.

I trip down the steps, nearly causing myself to tumble down them headfirst, but I grip the railing and keep going. The man at the next level looks up at my panicked exit, but the blood is pounding too loudly in my ears for me to hear what he says.

I don't know if I'm expecting some kind of emergency siren to sound, like I'm an intruder who must be stopped, but nothing does. I reach the front door without breaking an ankle.

"Keys. I need my keys. And my car. Now. Hurry. It's an emergency."

The man straightens with a jerk and nods before opening the door and giving an instruction into what must be a microphone attached to his collar.

I shove my feet into my heels, then stumble down the last set of steps to the curved driveway, chancing a glance over my shoulder.

Is he going to chase me?

Do I want him to?

I can't afford to let myself answer that last question as I hustle down to the valet stand.

I keep checking over my shoulder, expecting the door to burst open any moment, but it doesn't. My Bronco rumbles around the corner and the valet hops out.

I practically clobber him in my rush to get inside. Trembling, I slam the door in his face and floor it.

What the hell did I do?

CHAPTER 3

Temperance

THE QUESTION HAUNTS ME ALL THE WAY HOME, still echoing in my head when I find a spot on the street in the French Quarter and throw the Bronco into park. My confusion dogs my heels as I walk toward the old iron gate that separates me from the passageway that connects to the courtyard outside my tiny second-floor apartment.

His perfect body and tattoos are flashing through my mind as my heels click on the brick. My heart still thuds in uneven beats, and I wonder if it's possible to have permanent heart palpitations from the best sex of your life.

Small price to pay, I think before quashing the thought.

But I can't ignore the fact I can still feel him between my legs.

Why did I do it? Why didn't I run? It's not like he

wove a spell on me and hypnotized me with his dick.

That didn't happen until a bit later. A half whimper, half chuckle escapes from my lips as I reach the courtyard.

"That you, Temperance?"

My gaze searches the darkness, interrupted only by the Chinese lanterns and fairy lights hanging from the trees and the watery blue light coming from the splash pool, until it lands on the red dragon emblazoned on the back of a black silk kimono, topped by a fluffy white head of hair.

Shit. My landlady.

"I'm so sorry to disturb you, Harriet. I'll just—"

She spins around, spry for her advanced age. "Oh, girl, you've got sex hair. At least that makes one of us."

I squeeze my eyes shut in humiliation. "I . . . uh . . . got—"

"Done up right by a real man, I'd say. About damn time, girl. I was starting to think you were a lost cause of all work and no play. Almost wondered if I'd have to find a new tenant to get some entertainment around here."

I blink twice as she shuffles toward me, fluffy pink marabou slippers on her feet. "You were going to kick me out because I work too much?"

I knew my landlady was a little nutty, but I didn't realize she was downright crazy.

"It would've been a last resort. I was going to

send you a male stripper first. Girl, you need some fun in your life, and you do nothing but go between here and work. Boring as hell."

Her point is finally sinking in, but part of me is still in shock. "I'm boring?"

"Of course you are. I swear, you go out of your way to stay that way too. But not tonight. Tonight, you look like you got dicked down by a real man." She takes a seat at the outdoor patio table and reaches for a bottle of wine. "Here's a glass. Now, sit down and consider part of your rent spilling the juicy details."

Dumbstruck, I close the distance between us and take a seat at the table. "It's nothing. I swear."

"Girl, you're practically walking bowlegged. I've been around the block plenty of times. You won't shock me."

I reach for the glass of wine and take a long drink. *Good Lord, I needed this.*

"I shouldn't even be admitting what I did tonight."

Harriet's aged eyes practically light up as she grins. "Those are the *best* stories. Come now, I'll take it to the grave."

I squeeze my eyes shut. "I think I accidentally went to a sex club."

Harriet's wineglass clinks the metal of the table. "I knew this was going to be good. How do you *accidentally* go to a sex club?"

I tell her about the note that came to the office, and rushing to meet the appointment, assuming I was there to sell whiskey . . . and end with the part about running from the room.

Harriet claps with childlike excitement. "There's hope for you yet, Temperance. When are you going back?"

I'm stunned at her reaction. I didn't exactly expect her to judge, but I sure didn't think she'd cheer me on.

"Never. I can't. That's not me. I'm not . . ."

"Interesting? Sexually adventurous? Up to be manhandled regularly by a real man?"

"I don't even know his name!"

Harriet waves off my concern. "If I had a nickel for every man whose name I didn't know, I'd be even richer than I am now. You can't take life so seriously. You'll never make it out alive. Now, you go upstairs, take the rest of this bottle of wine, and get tipsy enough to forget all the shouldn'ts and can'ts. If you need me to do some stalking to find this guy, just let me know. I have *connections*."

I can't even begin to imagine what kind of connections Harriet, an elderly artist who has lived in New Orleans for decades, could possibly have, but I wouldn't put anything past her.

If she told me she was besties with the Queen of England, I wouldn't be all that surprised.

I reach for the bottle, intending to pour her

another glass, but she stops me.

"Don't worry, I have a second one chilling. Go run along and drink. If you want to skinny-dip later, you're more than welcome. I'll be in my studio until dawn."

A sharp pang of envy lances through me at the thought of spending time in a studio, creating something from nothing.

One more thing I shouldn't be thinking about.

I don't have room in my life for that either anymore.

I grab the bottle of wine by the neck and give her a smile. "Good night, Harriet."

"*Bonne nuit*, Temperance."

CHAPTER 4

Temperance

HAVEN'T BEEN ABLE TO STOP THINKING ABOUT Friday night, and not just because I can feel him with my every step. No other experience in my life comes remotely close.

And I have absolutely no idea who he is or how to get in contact with him.

That's probably a good thing. Right?

He's still on my mind when I walk into the distillery on Monday morning. As soon as I turn the key, the heat, humidity, and scents wash over me. This is familiar. Sane. Not impulsive and crazy.

I've made a career for myself. A name for myself. Within these walls, I have respect, and no one questions that I deserve it. I'm not some girl from the bayou, running wild and trying to survive despite the shitty hand life dealt me.

As my heels click on the old concrete floor, I

remind myself that even though whiskey isn't my passion, this is the right path for me. It doesn't matter that I spend more time here than I do in my own apartment. This job is a privilege that I'm doing my best to prove I deserve.

Going off the deep end and letting my wild side come back to life isn't going to help me prove a damn thing except I've lost my mind. I have to put him out of my head.

No more club.

No more beautiful tattooed man.

No more getting off track.

I turn the handle of my office door and freeze when I see the lamp on my desk already lit, and thick-soled leather boots resting on my calendar.

What the hell? My hand automatically reaches for the gun in my purse.

"Shoot me, and you're gonna be the one to patch me up."

My brother's distinctive voice halts my movements in a way nothing else could.

"What the hell are you doing here? Get your damn boots off my desk. You can't be here."

I can't even imagine how the hell Rafe got inside. My boss's husband has this place locked down tighter than Fort Knox. Or maybe the Tower of London. After all, Keira is his crown jewel.

Rafe's boots stay exactly where they are. "I can't come ask my little sister if she's lost her goddamn mind? Because that's the only reason I can come up with for you to be at Haven."

"Haven?" The word comes off my tongue as though it's foreign.

He slides his boots off my desk, leaving traces of mud on my calendar that make me itch to slap him silly.

I've worked too damn hard to not leave a mess everywhere I go, but Rafe is a different story. He'll never be anything but a bayou boy, and he doesn't see a damn thing wrong with it. Hell, he's proud of the fact.

"Don't pretend like you don't know, girl."

I glance down at my watch. "I don't have time to pretend. I have a meeting with my boss starting in an hour, and I have two hours of work to get done to prep for it."

"Then maybe you should've worked this week-end instead of spending time at a sex club."

My mouth drops open as shock ricochets through my system. "Are you having me watched?"

He shrugs. "I ain't got time to babysit you, Tempe, regardless of how much you apparently need it."

"Who told you?"

Rafe eyes me. "Doesn't matter. What matters is whether you've lost your damn mind. I don't care how high-and-mighty you think you are these days, there are some places you don't belong, and Haven is one of them. There are some bad motherfuckers that go there to get their kink on, and I'm not talking about people like us. I'm talking about the rich and powerful kind who would chew you up and toss you out with the trash."

His warning hits me hard. "I don't know what you're talking about."

"And you shouldn't. Ever. Stay away from that place and anyone you see coming or going outta there."

I plant my hands on my hips. "And how do you know so much about this place?"

"Don't matter, but the fact that I do should warn you off even more."

I roll my eyes because I've gotten this lecture a dozen times. My brother definitely falls under the category of *bad motherfucker*. He doesn't live on the right side of the law on his best day. I'm not sure he ever has. One more reason why having him in my office is less than ideal, regardless of the fact my boss's husband *is* the wrong side of the law.

"I'm not talking about this with you. So, if that's all the reason you have to be here, feel free to see yourself out the way you came in."

Rafe hauls himself out of my chair and stomps across the room. "Tempe, you're better than that shit. Better than those people. You've got a life here. A respectable one that you've busted your ass for, because God knows, you've lorded it over me plenty. You want to lose everything? Then keep associating with the people at Haven."

I meet his dark brown eyes, eyes that mirror mine. "I don't need you telling me what to do anymore. I'm doing just fine on my own."

His jaw tenses like he wants to strangle me. I recognize the look and ignore it. After a few long seconds of a staring contest, he lets out a sigh.

"Look, you're all I got left. You expect me not to worry about my baby sister, then you're fucking crazy."

"I'm fine."

He snorts. "You're not fine, Tempe. You ain't been fine in a long while. But I ain't got time to fix that right now. I gotta go. I got a job. A big one."

Rafe never speaks to me about work, so for him to bring it up, especially here, means this isn't just a big job, it's a *big job*. A chill works its way up my spine because I know Rafe's line of work isn't the kind where you're guaranteed to make it home safe and sound.

"Where? What?"

He tilts his head to the right. "You know better than to ask that kind of shit."

"How long? When will you be back?"

He reaches out and flips the end of my hair. "You know I won't miss your birthday, so before then sometime."

The uneasiness building inside me subsides a bit. "You're sure?"

His hand claps around on my shoulder. "Damn sure. But you gotta promise me one thing."

"What?"

"Trust your gut. If something seems off, tell Mount. Don't hesitate. He'll know what to do."

A chill snakes down my spine like someone just walked over my grave. Maybe because Rafe has never told me to go to anyone else for help. Ever.

"Rafe . . ."

"It'll be okay. We're always okay, aren't we?" He yanks me in for a hard hug. "Don't go reminiscing about your wild-child days either. You got an itch to scratch, go out on a date with a banker or a lawyer or something. Stay the fuck away from Haven."

I squeeze him hard. "Don't tell me what to do. Just come back safe."

"Always do."

He releases me and I watch him walk out of my office, my unease climbing with his every step.

Lord, keep him safe. He's all I've got left.

CHAPTER 5

Temperance

"K NOCK, KNOCK." I RAP ON THE WOODEN doorjamb of my boss's office fifty-eight minutes later, injecting a cheerful note into my voice.

Keira, my blindingly gorgeous redhead of a boss, smiles when she sees me. "Hey, Temperance. I was just about to order breakfast. You want your usual?"

I don't turn down food. Maybe it's because I went to bed with my stomach growling too many times as a kid, or maybe because I'm perpetually hungry. Either way, my answer is a foregone conclusion.

"Absolutely."

Keira's lips, slicked red, curve into a smile, and for a second, I'm reminded of the masked woman Friday night. *The woman I watched . . .*

I need to block that out and pretend it never

happened, but the vivid memories make it nearly impossible.

Thankfully, Keira doesn't notice my hesitation, because she's already on the phone to place our typical breakfast order.

I settle into a guest chair in front of her desk with my notebook on my lap. It's full of checklists and final details that we have to run through before the big fundraiser Seven Sinners is hosting on Thursday night for Mary's House, a local women's shelter.

After our successful Mardi Gras party for the Voodoo Kings football team, word spread that Seven Sinners is the perfect place to hold high-profile events that need extra panache. Now we're up to our eyeballs in requests, and my job, which was already busy, has taken over my life completely, leaving no time for anything else.

That's why it didn't even occur to me to question meeting a potential customer on a Friday night. Even though I should dig to the bottom of how the hell the mix-up occurred, I'm far too embarrassed to admit what I did.

Over and done with.

Never to be thought of again.

Except in the dark of my room late at night.

This event-planning aspect of my job wasn't exactly what I signed up for, but it's not like I was going to say no to Keira. She's a great boss, and being promoted to COO of Seven Sinners is more than I ever expected when I hired on as an office assistant.

When Keira hangs up, she smiles at me again. "So, what do we need to tackle first?"

"Donors will begin dropping off auction pieces today. If it's okay with you, I'll just keep them all in my office so there's no chance of them getting misplaced or damaged." To myself, I add, *especially because my brother won't be popping in for any more visits for a bit.* The same feeling of unease creeps through me, but I push it away.

"Good idea. Keep a log of them as we receive them, and we'll move everything upstairs once the final preparations for the room are in place."

"Got it." I move down to the next item on my list. "Odile has asked me to confirm for the third time that we have the correct estimated number of attendees."

Keira winces. "I got an email over the weekend from the president that they have some heavy hitters who RSVP'd late, and they're too big of potential donors to turn down."

"Okay, so we need to increase by a few?"

"Try fifteen or twenty."

I can already imagine the head chef of Seven Sinners chasing me out of the kitchen with a butcher knife when I relay that information. "So, you want to talk to Odile about that this afternoon?"

Keira laughs. "If you're scared of her . . ."

"It's not her, it's her close proximity to sharp

objects that I'm afraid of." I pause, reminding myself it's my job, so I need to handle it. "But it's not a problem. I'm sure she'll be thrilled to accommodate the changes."

The snort-laugh that follows is pretty much the only appropriate reaction. "Right. Totally. She'll be thrilled. I'll let Mary's House know the extra attendees won't be a problem, but they will see an increase in the final bill."

"Damn right they will," I mumble, thinking of the gauntlet I'm going to run on their behalf as I make another note on my pad.

"Oh, and I totally forgot to ask if you wanted to bring a date," Keira says. "You know you can, even though it's a work event." My face must freeze in some unflattering expression, because she laughs. "Or not."

I force my lips into some semblance of a smile, and my brain stutters as I try to come up with something to say in response besides *hell no.* "I'm . . . uh . . . that's really not necessary."

"You're going to make me think I'm working you so hard you don't have any time left for fun at all. What about Jeff Doon? He asked me if you were seeing anyone after that interview for the local network about the distillery tours."

"Jeff Doon? The guy from the chamber of commerce?" I ask like I don't know who he is, mostly to buy myself some time to overcome my shock. I never would have expected him to show any interest in me, considering he was Keira's high school boyfriend.

"It's not weird, I promise. He was so impressed with how you've spearheaded the tour project and wondered if you might want to grab a drink with him sometime, but apparently he felt the need to ask for my blessing first."

"I'm not sure what to say. I . . . I don't really date, I guess." It's a true statement, especially because what happened Friday night was definitely not a date. But that's not something I can ever tell my boss about. "Besides, I'm still fending off advances from the meat supplier because of the promises I made him to get the Voodoo Kings the cuts they wanted at the price we had to quote."

Keira giggles at that one. "If you ever go out with him, I promise I'll award you hazard pay for it. That's above and beyond the call of duty."

"I've held him off for this long with excuses, but for some reason, that hasn't discouraged him nearly enough."

Keira's head tilts to the left. "In the sage words of the wise Magnolia Maison, have you looked in the mirror lately, girl? Because you're shit hot."

I choke out a laugh. "I think you're talking about yourself."

She shrugs. "You need to get out. Do something. It'll appease my guilt about you working too many hours as it stands . . . and I'm going to be asking you to take the reins again because my husband has decided we're taking a vacation."

I sit up in the chair. "When?"

"He wants to leave next week. I told him I'll see how it goes with the event and—"

"It's fine. I can handle things. You know I can." It's a matter of pride for me to know that Keira can leave her company in my hands and disappear for a few days without worrying about it burning to the ground.

"I'll tell him I'm thinking about it. I can't give in to him right away because then he'll think he's got the upper hand. It's all about methods and tactics with that man." Keira's phone rings and she grabs it. "Keira Kilgore."

I can't hear the voice coming through the other end, but it doesn't take long before I can guess.

"Don't you dare. And we agreed I would use the Kilgore name as long as Seven Sinners is around."

Lachlan Mount, her husband.

Does he know my brother was here? It doesn't take a rocket scientist to assume that he knows exactly who I am and who Rafe is and what he does. Mount knows everything, after all.

It's just one more reason I need to watch my step and make sure Rafe's job doesn't spill over into mine.

"Yes, I'm still thinking about the vacation. No, you can't hurry my decision."

I look at the ceiling, not wanting to feel like I'm intruding on Keira's conversation. Thankfully, there's a knock at the door, and I pop out of my chair to answer it.

Breakfast.

"Breakfast is here, which I'm sure you already know, so let me call you back after this meeting. Yes. I love you too."

Keira hangs up as I return to her desk with the bags containing our food.

"Men. I swear." She rolls her eyes, but I know she finds comfort in his overprotective nature.

Either way, I can't imagine having a man look at me the way Mount looks at her. Like he'd kill anyone who made her frown. And, honestly, he might.

"You should go on the vacation. I can handle things."

With a smile, she digs into her grits. "I know you can, Temperance. That was never in doubt."

"Then why the cat-and-mouse game with him?"

Her smile turns sly. "Because that's how you have to handle a man like Lachlan Mount. Otherwise, he'd bulldoze right over me. Besides, my spitfire ways keep him on his toes."

Her words rattle around in my brain as we eat and discuss the remaining items on the never-ending to-do list, and I keep myself from thinking about my stranger.

He had that same demeanor that screamed *I take*

what I want. He'd be a bulldozer. *And I'd like it.*

Just as quickly, I push the thought out of my brain and bury it six feet under.

I'm never going to see him again, so it doesn't matter.

CHAPTER 6

Temperance

G UESTS ARE DUE TO START ARRIVING IN THIRTY minutes and my office looks like it's been ransacked. Crates and packing material are scattered everywhere, thanks to all the auction pieces that have been unwrapped and transported upstairs.

Well, not quite all.

I roll my eyes as I glance at the open crate labeled EXTREMELY FRAGILE—BREAK IT AND YOU DIE. Gregor Standish, the artist who donated it, has been a pain in my ass since the day he decided to get involved with this Mary's House event. As grateful as I am that we're going to raise even more money because of his contribution, part of me wishes he would just come pick up the monstrosity. It looks like a cactus made of blobs of yellow wax left out in the sun too long.

New Orleans Rising, he calls it.

It looks like New Orleans melting, if you ask me, but then again, what do I know? The kind of art I like isn't what inspires people to gather in groups and talk about how it makes them question their existential crisis, not that I know what that means either.

My kind of art is raw and obvious. The kind that lacks subtlety and punches you in the gut when you see it. Maybe that's because I wasn't raised sophisticated enough to be the existential-crisis type.

My gaze shifts to the sculpture in the opposite corner of my office—one that won't be in the auction because no one would ever ask its artist to donate. The fleur de lis stands five feet tall, made of welded reclaimed metal objects.

Junk art. At least, that's what my daddy used to call my creations. I can still hear his voice telling me that we'd be better off getting the scrap money from the metal than letting me play with it.

Just one more reason it's hard to be sad he's gone.

I turn away from the crate and the sculpture and reach for the dress hanging on the back of my door. It wouldn't do for the COO of Seven Sinners to arrive in a blouse covered in smudges of dust and dirt from all the manual labor I put in this afternoon ensuring every piece was perfectly arranged upstairs.

But, of course, I'm not allowed to move *New Orleans Rising* until the artist, Gregor Standish, arrives tonight, and he's late.

Putting Mr. Standish's problem with punctuality

out of my mind for two minutes, I kick off my shoes, adjust my thigh-highs, and pull the little black dress, flattering yet completely professional, off the hanger.

I step into it and reach around for the zipper. It's about three inches above my ass when my arm cramps and someone knocks on my office door, the door I didn't remember to lock before stripping to change.

"Shit," I whisper, hopping on one foot and attempting to contort my arm so I can reach the zipper I've lost my grip on. "Hold on, please."

The door opens and a man sticks his head inside.

"Oh. So sorry. I didn't mean to catch you in a state of undress."

It's Ronnie Lyle, another donor for the fundraiser's auction, who gave me the creeps earlier this week when he dropped off his nude painting. Not that I have anything against nudes, just this guy.

"If you could please step out for a moment, Mr. Lyle, I'll be right with you."

His half smile widens, and my creep-o-meter climbs. "Or I could give you a hand with that zipper you seem not to be able to reach. After all, that's what a gentleman would do."

"I've got it."

"I'm sure you do, but everyone could use an extra hand now and again." He steps inside my office and closes the door.

Gritting my teeth to keep my placid expression

in place, I have to force myself not to tell him to open the door right this second. If he tries to make a move, I'll break his fingers.

"I appreciate your *gentlemanly* offer." I almost choke on the words, but he doesn't seem to hear anything after I give him my back. Probably hasn't seen a woman in a state of undress in the last decade. Then again, he flaunts his money and power, so I'm probably wrong. *Blech.*

His shoes scuff on the concrete floor as he strides closer, and I tense with every scrape.

"You're a very beautiful woman, Ms. Ransom," he says, and I do my best not to cringe.

His breath on my ear gives me the urge to bolt, but I keep my stocking-covered feet firmly in place. I won't give him the satisfaction of knowing that he creeps me out so much. That would give him too much power, and I refuse to allow it.

The zipper begins to inch its way upward, but he stops around the area where the band of my bra would be.

"You know, I have a limo coming to pick me up after the event, and I'd be happy to take you—"

I whip around, yanking the zipper out of his hold and reaching behind my back to tug it up the last couple of inches.

"I got it from here. Thanks so much. Feel free to show yourself upstairs. The bar should be serving shortly."

My office door opens again.

"Temperance, did you need help . . ." Keira's voice trails off when she realizes I'm not alone—and not wearing any shoes. "Mr. Lyle, I didn't realize you had business with Ms. Ransom. Is there something I can help you with?"

Lyle steps back and clears his throat. "No. Not at all. I was just telling Ms. Ransom what a wonderful job y'all have done so far, and how excited I am to see what kind of money Mary's House is able to raise to help those poor women."

The lies roll off his tongue so easily, making my creep-o-meter ding again like someone hit the jackpot.

"I'm sure it will be absolutely fabulous," Keira says, and I can't help but wonder if she senses my unease. "Would you like to accompany me up to the restaurant so you can personally taste the Phoenix label I know you've been wanting to purchase? I think Ms. Ransom would like some privacy so she can finish getting ready."

Lyle turns back to me and his gaze traces my body. "Of course. I'll see you soon, Ms. Ransom."

CHAPTER 7

Temperance

'M WORKING THE CROWD WITH A SMILE AS GUESTS partake in Seven Sinners' best whiskey, but inside I'm having a minor meltdown. Ronnie Lyle keeps trying to corner me, Gregor Standish hasn't shown up yet, and the auction starts in ten minutes.

Leaving the crowded restaurant, I slip into the alcove near the bathroom where the noise of conversations is muted to a dull roar and pull out my cell phone to call him again.

It goes straight to voice mail.

"Where the hell is he?"

Spinning around, I search the room for Keira. I need to update her on the situation so we can make a decision.

I catch a glimpse of a face in the crowd that freezes my feet to the floor while it sends a pulse of heat through my body.

I know that mouth. That jawline. Those broad-set shoulders.

No. Impossible. My mind is playing tricks.

There's no way the guy from the club can be here.

I blink twice, staring at him—until he turns and his icy blue eyes lock with mine. Shock and recognition flit across his face.

No. This can't be happening. Goose bumps pebble along my skin as he surveys me, his gaze traveling down my body before returning to my face. One corner of his mouth lifts, and an expression that looks a lot like satisfaction settles on his features.

Is this a setup? Is he going to approach me? What the hell am I going to say?

My phone buzzes, and I'm torn out of the staring contest I've been unwittingly dragged into by the stranger who I let fuck me within the first fifteen minutes of meeting him.

Classy, Temperance.

I look down at the phone and breathe a sigh of relief when I read Gregor's number. "Mr. Standish?"

The response is garbled and impossible to decipher.

"Sir?"

Something that sounds like *office* comes through my phone, and I hope like hell he's telling me he's down in my office. I step forward, my gaze automatically cutting back to where the stranger was standing, but he's gone.

Was he really here? Or have I moved on to full-blown hallucinations as a result of the orgasms he gave me?

I move through the crowd toward the stairwell, trying to speak with Mr. Standish, but his phone is cutting out in the middle of every other word. Cell service is crap in the basement where my office is, so I hope that means he's down there.

The call drops as soon as I reach the middle of the crowd.

Hell.

I excuse myself at least a dozen times as I make my way to the stairway. I push open the door and grab the rail to race down the first flight of stairs. When I reach the landing, the stairwell door behind me slams shut.

"Running off again?" There's no mistaking that deep, rasping voice.

"You," I whisper.

His mobile mouth quirks into something that would barely qualify as a smile, and I absorb the impact of his face without a mask. Not classically handsome, but rugged and raw in the same way that I like my art. His masculine features lack subtlety, and they're a punch to the gut.

"Me, indeed." He takes the stairs almost lazily, stopping when he's standing before me on the landing.

My nipples approve of his tall form and perfectly

tailored suit, but my brain still can't comprehend what's happening. "What are you doing here?"

"What do you think?"

"I have no idea, but I'm—"

"Running again, like I said. Seems to be a talent of yours."

"No. I have business to take care of."

"Maybe I do too."

Those blue eyes heat, and the expression on his face says he'd just as soon fuck me up against the concrete stairwell as do anything businesslike.

"You can't be here. You have to leave."

"Says who? Maybe I was invited, *Ms. Smith*."

I've been over the guest list dozens of times, but not since Keira added the late RSVPs. Can he be one of them? What are the odds?

But hearing the name he called me that night stops me short. "I tried to tell you I wasn't her."

He steps closer, crowding me as he presses a palm to the wall beside my head. "I didn't give a damn who you were after watching you watch them."

"I wasn't—" I say quickly, trying to deny it.

"Don't waste your breath lying about it. It was sexy as fuck. Just like you."

Heat zings from my nipples to my clit at the hunger in his gaze. I've convinced myself it was just the club itself and watching the couple that made our encounter so explosive, but now I know I'm wrong.

It's him. This man wears raw power and

confidence easier than he does his suit jacket.

"I can't do this here. Not now."

"Do what? We're just talking."

"I'm at work."

He raises an eyebrow. "What about later?"

It's a struggle to fight my body's reaction. To fight the urge to reach out and press my palm to his hard chest. To remember why I have to hurry the rest of the way down these stairs.

"I can't. That night . . . it was a mistake."

He presses his other palm to the wall, caging me between his strong arms. But instead of feeling trapped, my body is staging a mutiny and urging me to wrap myself around him.

God, he smells so good.

I force my reactions down and curl my hands into fists to keep from touching him.

"A mistake? Is that what you're telling yourself? Because I remember it differently—a beautiful woman bending to my command so I could turn her ass red before I fucked her and made her come so hard, I thought her pussy was going to strangle my cock."

Oh my God. His words are like fuel on the fire raging inside me, and I can't form a coherent response.

He lowers his head and skims his lips along my forehead to my ear. "I haven't been able to stop thinking about it."

Unable to respond, I haul in a shaky breath.

"Meet me again. Tonight."

My chin jerks up so I can meet his fierce gaze. "But—"

"Say *yes*, dammit, and I swear you won't regret it."

"I can't."

Those icy blue eyes snap with energy. "You can, and you want to." He drops one arm and pulls something from his pocket.

A business card.

He presses it into my hand. "I'll see you tonight."

He backs away, holding my stare hostage until he turns to climb the stairs and return to the fundraiser. I'm still frozen in place when he disappears through the door.

What the hell is wrong with me? I didn't even ask his name.

More than anything, I want to chase after him, but—*Standish.*

Shit. I shove the card into my bra and run.

When I reach my office, there's no sign of the artist there, in the hallway or out in the parking lot. The valets confirm they haven't seen a man matching his description.

Just freaking great.

My phone buzzes with a text.

Keira: Auction is starting. Where are you?

Crap.

I tap out a reply.

TEMPERANCE: *On my way.*

I rush to the elevator and ride it up to the top floor. When I step out, I hear the bidding frenzy in process for the first piece.

Standish is shit out of luck, and I'm not taking the blame.

Numbers roll off the auctioneer's tongue like water off a duck's back as I weave through the crowd to find my boss and explain why Gregor Standish's sculpture isn't on the auction block first.

When I glance up at the stage, I halt in mid-step.

Oh sweet Lord. This is not happening.

There's a sculpture on the stage, but it's not the melty yellow blob.

No.

It's mine.

CHAPTER 8

Temperance

"**D**O I HAVE TWENTY THOUSAND?" THE auctioneer asks, and paddles pop into the air as bids are called. It rises to thirty. Then forty. Then forty-five.

All the blood must have drained from my head, because I feel like I'm going to pass out. The bids slow and the auctioneer calls it.

"*Sold* . . . to bidder number thirty-seven for $50,000. Congratulations, sir. Next up, we have—"

My ears tune out the rest of what he's saying as I search the crowd for number thirty-seven, but I don't see the paddle anymore, or people congratulating the victorious bidder.

Who in the world would pay fifty thousand for my sculpture? This can't be happening.

My stomach tumbles like it's full of hopping bullfrogs, but I push forward through the crowd to find

Keira. She's standing off to the side of the stage, and her tall, dark, and handsome husband stands behind her.

When she sees me, her expression is pained.

Oh shit. Shit. Shit. Now I'm going to get fired.

"I don't know what happened," I whisper as soon as I get closer. "Standish called, and I was trying to track him down, and . . . I have no idea how that got up there."

Instead of giving me a disapproving stare, Keira winces. "I am so, so sorry."

"What?"

"It's my fault. The auctioneer told me we were missing the first auction item, so I told the crew to get the last sculpture, whether Standish was here or not. They brought up the one from your office, and I didn't realize their mistake until it was already onstage and the auctioneer launched into bidding. Maybe we can get it back? Explain the situation and cancel the bid?"

"Are you joking? If someone wants to pay fifty thousand dollars for that, do you really think I'm going to stop them? Especially when it goes to such a good cause?"

"Are you sure? I'll pay to replace it for you. I swear."

My head jerks back in shock, but before I can reply to Keira's offer, a gorgeous woman with long black hair taps her on the shoulder.

"You've got to tell me who the artist was for that piece. I got outbid, but I know for a fact that was not a Gregor Standish."

And here it comes. Because there's no way anyone could mistake my reclaimed metal art for a Gregor Standish.

"There's no way in hell I would've bid that high for one of his melted-crayon-looking things."

Shock bubbles up inside me, and I'm speechless.

Keira glances from the woman to me. "You'll have to ask Temperance. She coordinated the auction, and that piece was a last-minute swap that went out mislabeled. We're going to inform the buyer and let him know about the mistake to see if he wants to cancel his bid."

The woman extends a hand and I shake it automatically. "I'm Valentina Hendrix. I own Noble Art, and if the winner cancels his bid, I'll match it. I want the piece and the artist's name."

Somehow, I keep my jaw from dropping at her declaration. Noble Art is one of the top galleries in the Quarter, and so prestigious and expensive, I've never done more than peer through the windows from the sidewalk.

"Temperance?" Keira prompts me when I don't say anything in reply.

I find my tongue and ability to lie. "I believe the artist was anonymous. I don't have a name to give you."

One of Valentina's perfect dark eyebrows goes up. "Anonymous. Hmm." She surveys me with a look I can't interpret. "I've heard that story before."

Shit. She knows I'm lying. "Excuse me, but I need to go find the buyer and explain that there's been a mistake."

"Keep me posted, Temperance. My offer stands."

Shell-shocked, I weave through the crowd again, mumbling *excuse me* over and over because I don't know what else to say.

Tonight couldn't have gone more differently than I expected if the entire building had disappeared into a sinkhole.

I slide around the side of the stage we set up for the auction and try to catch the attention of an auctioneer's assistant who's in charge of moving the items. He holds up a finger before carrying out the third piece.

When he returns, he steps off the stage as the auctioneer begins his spiel. "Can I help you?"

"Who bought the first piece? I need to speak with him or her."

The guy shrugs. "It was a man, but I'm not sure who. We've got the payment table set up in the corner. Maybe you can catch him there."

Duh. Why didn't I think of that?

Probably because my brain is already fried tonight from too many curveballs.

"Thanks."

I make my way to the opposite corner of the room where a table is set up for the payment of donations. The man sitting there glances up at me from a stack of paperwork.

"I need to speak to whomever bought the first piece before he pays."

"Too late. Already got his payment."

"His? What did he look like?"

The man blinks behind glasses as thick as Coke bottles. "Well, I can't exactly say. It was a man."

"Older than you? Younger? Gray hair? Purple?"

His expression turns disapproving. "I'm afraid I didn't catalog his attributes, but I do have a check if that helps."

He opens a folder and pulls it out. I snatch it out of his hand.

"Nunya Holdings LLC?"

"Yes, and he's sending someone to pick up the item tomorrow morning. Said he couldn't take it this evening."

"Thank you."

As I turn away from the table, my phone vibrates again and I look down.

Gregor Standish.

Oh good Lord. I wonder if he heard a sculpture that wasn't his was auctioned in his place. He's going to want my head on a platter.

I send the call to voice mail.

He can wait until tomorrow.

CHAPTER 9

Temperance

Keira's waiting in my office when I finish clearing out the restaurant after the event. We both look at the uncrated yellow monstrosity.

"Did Standish call you?" I ask.

She nods. "Only eight times. I sent them all to voice mail."

"I'm so sorry."

"It's not your fault. In fact, it wouldn't have happened if he'd shown up on time. If he gives us any kind of issue . . . well, you know that will go over like a lead balloon."

"I can imagine," I say wryly. If Standish were to look cross-eyed at Keira, I doubt he'd ever make another sculpture again. "It's probably better if I deal with him. We wouldn't want him going missing or anything."

She laughs, but we both know it's not that much

of a joke. "Did you find the bidder?"

I shake my head. "Not exactly. But I have the name of his company. He's supposed to arrange pickup tomorrow. I'll find him and give him the option to take the real piece or to cancel the bid."

"And if he doesn't go for it?"

I look over my shoulder at the melted cactus. "Then Standish can come get his masterpiece and take it home."

Keira laughs. "I swear, I'll never understand modern art. Honestly, I think your sculpture was a hundred times cooler. Plus, it didn't remind me of a mustard mishap."

Warmth curls inside my belly at her words. I know she means "my sculpture" only because I owned it, but I still hold the compliment close.

"Thanks."

"I'm really sorry I screwed that up. If you can find another, I'll pay to replace it."

My lips press hard together. "Not necessary."

"I mean it. It's the least I can do."

"I don't think there's another, but I appreciate the offer." Wanting to change the subject, I add, "I'll let you know when I get in touch with the buyer and deal with Standish."

She gives me a kind smile. "Just so you know, I'm interviewing for more help after this vacation. I know event planning isn't your favorite thing, so I'm going to look for someone to handle it."

A pit of worry forms in my belly. "Oh . . . Okay. I hope you don't think I'm doing a crap job."

"Definitely not. Don't think that. I'm well aware that you're buried beneath a thousand pounds of work right now, and I've relied on you because you're like me—you keep pushing through, no matter what. You can only do it for so long before you burn out, and I don't want that for you."

"Oh, thank you. I appreciate that."

"You can head out. I'll handle the rest of this stuff tonight. You've worked your ass off on this event. Maybe go have some fun for once."

"Are you sure?"

Keira nods. "Absolutely."

"Okay, then. I won't argue." I grab my purse from my desk drawer, and the order I was given comes to life in my head as soon as Keira waves me off and I reach my car.

"Meet me again. Tonight."

I unlock my Bronco and climb inside. For a fraction of a second, I consider turning away from town toward the winding country road that would bring me to the gate and the mansion.

But I turn right instead.

I make it through three lights before I whip my car around, pulling a U-turn in the middle of the road to the sound of blaring horns.

CHAPTER 10

Temperance

MY ANTICIPATION CLIMBS WITH EVERY MILE that passes—along with the feeling that I'm insane. But that doesn't stop my body from humming with nervous, excited energy.

I shouldn't be doing this. I know that better than I know my own name.

I don't make reckless choices anymore. I've worked too hard to get my life exactly where I need it to be to take risks.

Yes, I searched for clubs like this months ago. My curiosity was piqued after I heard some of the Voodoo Kings football players discussing where they were headed after their Mardi Gras bash. Later that same week, I caught the tail end of a conversation between two ladies at lunch who mentioned a place where identities were hidden and fantasies were fair game.

Two instances in one week made it beyond tempting, but my search for a place people like that would frequent came up empty. Would I have ever worked up the nerve to go if I'd discovered Haven?

Highly doubtful.

The most likely outcome would have been me climbing in bed with a dirty book and a toy, and making myself come before falling asleep.

What happened the other night *was* a mistake, even if the stranger doesn't believe that.

Girls like me can't afford to be reckless. We don't get that many chances, so screwing them up has harsher consequences.

So, what's my excuse for tonight? Craziness? Curiosity? A little of both?

I decide it doesn't matter as I give my name to whomever is at the other end of the speaker perched on a pole outside the gate. Now that I know what's hiding behind it, the wrought iron seems even more decadent.

Someone spared no expense making sure the outside is just as perfect as the inside. The trees are perfectly trimmed and the moss seems almost artfully draped. The muted glow of the lights lining the drive adds to the enticing allure. *Come,* it says. *Don't hesitate. You'll never find another place like this . . . and certainly not another man like* him.

The voice in my head is interrupted by reality.

"Welcome back, madam," the voice replies

through the speaker as the gate swings open.

My foot stays planted on the brake, and I consider what the hell I'm doing for the thousandth time since I whipped that U-turn.

Turn around, I tell myself. *Turn around and never look back. Forget this place and this man and go on with your safe little life.*

My brother's warning rings in my head about the kind of people who come here. Bad people. Does that make my stranger one of them? And even if he is . . . do I care?

I squeeze my eyes shut and another voice emerges, louder than the last.

You only get one life. Live the hell out of it. No regrets.

As the two options clash in my brain, the gates move again—this time to close and shut me out. Which would make my debate moot, because my choice is being stolen from me.

My hand, already on the gearshift, ready to throw my Bronco into reverse and retreat, is overridden by my gut. I punch the accelerator and my tires grab the pavement, rocketing me forward before the wrought-iron barrier can keep me from my destination.

Just one more time.

I'll steal one more night and walk away. I can do that. Rafe will never know. No one will but the stranger and me.

My resolve strengthened, I inhale several long,

deep breaths to steady myself as I slow the Bronco behind another car. A uniformed valet accepts the keys from a masked man climbing out of a white Mercedes, and a fraction of my nervous energy calms at the sight of another patron. At least for a moment, then another thought breaks through.

What if I see someone I recognize or who recognizes me? I need a mask, and it's not something I carry around in my Bronco. *Why didn't I think ahead?*

When the Mercedes pulls away, another masked man exits the front door and approaches my car. He's wearing a similar uniform to the valets and the doormen I saw last time, but his mask is a different color. He rounds the hood, and my nerves spike when he opens my door.

"Madam, I was informed that you might be in need of an accessory."

My mind, already halfway in the gutter by being in the proximity of the club, goes straight to the multitude of possible accessories to which he could be referring.

"Excuse me?" I ask, pulling away from the open door.

He regards me curiously as he pulls something silver from his inner breast pocket and holds it out. "Your mask, madam."

"Oh. Yes. Thank you." *What did you think he was going to offer you, Temperance? Nipple clamps?*

"If you'll step out and present your card, I'll help

you tie the mask and show you inside."

My card?

"Umm, one second." I turn away from the window and pull the card out of my bra—because I'm classy like that—and offer it to him.

"Thank you, ma'am."

I slide out of my Bronco and lean over to snag my purse and hook it over my shoulder. Taking the mask from him, I turn and give him my back. He deftly ties it on, and I adjust the positioning before facing him again.

"Please follow me, madam."

His avoidance of using my name sends a clear signal that anonymity is prized here, which is perfectly okay with me. Preferable, actually.

With a more confidence than I feel, I stride after the man, climbing the front steps. When the door opens, I'm once again transported to a different world.

Once inside, the thumping bass beat from the upper floor creates a slow, throbbing pulse that carries through the entire building, and I can't help but wonder if I'm going to see the inside of the room where it comes from tonight.

"I'll take care of her from here," says a familiar voice, a voice I don't want to hear here.

My gaze cuts to the woman standing just inside the foyer—my boss's best friend, Magnolia Maison.

Lord above, what are the odds? I don't answer my

own question because, really, why shouldn't I have expected to see the notorious madam in a sex club? I should almost have expected it, but I didn't. And now . . . she could tell my boss. *Great.*

I drop my head and pretend to cough so I can cover the bottom half of my face in a last-ditch effort to conceal my identity and avoid what will certainly be an awkward conversation with Keira.

"Ain't gonna work, *chérie.* We've got some talkin' to do." Magnolia crooks her finger. "Come on."

"But—" I protest, but she turns around and strolls out of the entryway.

Over her shoulder, she adds, "Don't worry. You're not gonna be late. He ain't here yet."

I swallow as my stomach flops. *How much does she know?* If I had to make a wager, I'd assume *everything.* Because that's how Magnolia operates.

She leads me down a hallway on the first floor into a richly appointed room that looks like it's half office and half boudoir. Gold-and-red wallpaper gives it a bold air, which suits Magnolia's personality, or at least what I know of it.

"Close the door behind you."

I push the wooden panel shut and lean against it, anchoring my purse to my side. "Please don't tell Keira I'm here. This doesn't have anything to do with work. It's . . . personal. And, honestly, I really don't want to have to explain any of this. You know?"

Magnolia turns away from my rambling pleas

and lifts a crystal decanter from a mirrored brass bar cart. From the scraps of information I've pieced together, I know Magnolia has been a madam for years, at least before an incident left her—and Keira and me—injured a few months ago.

I open my mouth again to fill the silence, intending to ask her how she's doing, but my lips seal shut when she speaks.

"Everything that happens here is *personal*, *chérie*." She looks over her shoulder at me as she replaces the stopper in the decanter. "Keira doesn't need to know anything. Her man either. I know how to keep a secret." An eerie feeling creeps up my spine as she turns and raises the tumbler to her red lips. "I'd offer you some, but we both know you'll decline."

Her statement—and knowledge of my drinking preferences—reinforces what I suspect is the God's honest truth. Magnolia Maison isn't someone I should underestimate.

She uses the glass to gesture at a leather chair with its back to an unlit fireplace. "Sit. Let's have ourselves a little chat."

I don't know why I'm obeying, but my feet move and I lower myself into the chair. Magnolia takes a brocade chaise longue. She sips the liquor and studies me.

"Who knows you're here?" she asks, not at all the question I expected.

"No one."

She tilts her head to the side. "When you're meeting a dangerous man, you should always let someone know where you're going. That's just being smart."

"Dangerous?"

"Oh, girl, you don't have a clue what you've gotten yourself into, do you?"

I think of the man who was at the distillery earlier tonight. The one who invited me back here again, and I couldn't resist.

Not wanting to sound as naive as I must appear, I straighten. "I can handle myself."

Magnolia smiles before throwing her head back and filling the room with rich laughter. "Lord, you're just as stubborn as Ke-ke. Once upon a time, I had to tell her how things worked. Didn't suspect I'd have to tell you. You should already know that people aren't always what they seem."

That eerie feeling returns. "What do you mean?"

"I know about you. Your people. Where you come from."

I stiffen, lifting my chin. "So?"

"Lock down your attitude, girl, I'm not here to threaten you. I'm here to help you."

"How?" I'm beginning to lose my patience.

"By giving you a helpful piece of advice. Keep whatever you've got going on here in the club. Don't take it outside. That's when things get dicey."

"Sounds like you don't think I should even be in the club."

She takes another drink before replying. "That's not at all what I'm saying. Come and fuck to your heart's content. I'm the last person who'll ever judge you for that. But you need to be careful. Be smart. Realize that this isn't your world, and you aren't equipped to handle the consequences of your actions if you take it outside the club. That man you're addicted to is smooth as hell but twice as dangerous."

A million questions surge to the forefront, but as I open my mouth to give voice to the first one, someone knocks on the door.

Magnolia glances toward it before meeting my gaze once more. "That's my next appointment. You ever need anything, you got my number. He should be here by now. Enjoy your night, Temperance. Be smart."

CHAPTER 11

Temperance

WITH MAGNOLIA'S WARNING DOGGING MY every step, I follow a man up the first flight of curving stairs.

I've worked hard to stay out of the danger that rules my brother's life, but apparently I went and stepped into something dangerous all on my own this time. After what she just told me, I should be walking out the front door, snatching my keys from the valet and flooring it down the drive without looking back.

But I'm not.

Magnolia's warning is having the opposite effect.

No part of me wants to flee. Instead, with every step I take toward this man—a dangerous man—my senses are heightened and my heart pounds.

I don't know what's wrong with me, but the edge of danger beckons me. Probably like a moth to a flame where I'll end up burned, but maybe that's what my life is missing. *Excitement. Risk.* Because I haven't been living. I've been existing.

Add on to that, there's a false sense of security that also stems from her warning. If I keep it within these walls, I can flirt with danger but not get hurt.

I'm not dumb enough to take big chances with my safety, but the thought of pushing the boundaries I've set for myself and *living* dumps a shot of adrenaline into my blood. After months of sleepwalking, I finally feel awake and alive.

As my escort brings me closer to where I assume my stranger is waiting, the memories of the last time I was here unfold in my mind and my blood heats.

By the time we stop in front of a door on the third level of the club, I've decided that Magnolia's warning isn't going to change a damn thing for me tonight. I want what this man can give me. I'll take it and walk away, no regrets.

"Enjoy, madam," my escort says before he leaves.

Enjoy? I'll do more than that. I'll revel.

With a secret smile on my face, I reach for the knob and turn it. The scent of old paper washes over me as I take in walls of books inside. *A library?*

Once again, there is only one lamp emitting a pool of light, this time over a pair of large leather chairs—both empty. But I know better than to assume I'm alone this time.

"Where are you?"

"I wondered if you'd come." His voice arises out of the shadows like it lives there. Belongs there. Like he belongs there.

Maybe I can too . . . for now.

I spin toward his voice, power filling me. "You doubted me?"

"I assumed you'd doubt yourself. Glad to see I was wrong. Drop your purse and turn around."

As soon as he delivers the order, the warnings and the worries fade away. *I need this.*

Because in this room, I don't have to be me, the responsible and respectable Temperance Ransom. I don't have to fret over doing the wrong thing or messing up. I'm not in charge here, and it's a heady feeling.

Especially because *he* is calling the shots.

I lower my purse to the floor and give him my back.

"Good girl." The approval in his voice washes over me. "Now, sit. Right chair."

I step around the chair and lower myself into it, my fingers gripping the cushioned arms.

The large black rectangle directly in front of me brightens like a television screen coming to life, but instead, it's a window into another room.

Another voyeur's paradise. My excitement rises until I realize what room I'm looking at.

It's the office we were in before.

"Oh my God. People watched us?" My voice

rises an octave as my heart rate skyrockets. I whip my head to the side, but I can't see him beyond the wide back of the chair I'm seated in.

"Would you have liked that?"

"I didn't have on a mask." My mind races, attempting to remember the layout of the room and where the window I'm viewing through could have been. "They would've seen—"

"Everything," he finishes for me, his voice coming closer. "But I don't like an audience. Not my style."

A relieved breath escapes my lips as I sink into the plush chair, my heart no longer feeling like it's going to explode.

"Thank God."

"But if they had . . ." His voice comes from just over my shoulder, and my spine stiffens as goose bumps rise on my exposed shoulders and arms. "What a fucking beautiful sight. You, bent over the desk. My handprint on your ass. Your sweet cunt on display as you spread your legs. The vision has been burned into my brain for days, but nothing makes me come harder than when I think about how you looked when you watched them. I need to watch you watch again."

Heat floods my system at his words, and doubles down when the door to the other room opens as the grandfather clock in the corner gongs the one o'clock hour.

I sit up straighter in the chair as a woman in a prim skirt suit, not unlike the one I wore the other night, enters the office followed by a man in slacks with his shirtsleeves rolled up over his forearms.

Watching my stranger—who I know in a biblical sense but not in any other way—roll up his shirtsleeves the other night over his thickly muscled, tattooed forearms was one of the most erotic sights I've experienced in my life. Actually, everything that happened in that office and everything I watched happen in the room beyond it makes that list.

I cross my legs tightly as the woman comes to a stop in front of the desk, and my movements take on more significance when I remember he is watching *me*. I turn to find where my watcher has decided to perch.

"Don't worry, I can see you just fine. Watch them." His voice has retreated once more to the shadows, but this time in the opposite corner of the room, where he must have a direct view of my chair but no vantage point to see what's happening in the office.

How the hell does he move so soundlessly? He's practically a ghost.

"It's different knowing you're here. I can't just forget that part."

A gravelly laugh is his response. "I dare you to try to forget me. Now, watch them."

I take his dare and tear my gaze away from his

outline in the darkness. I focus on the man unbuttoning his collar as he paces a half circle around the woman in front of him.

"You think I wouldn't notice the way you were touching yourself under the table in the meeting?" he says, already immersed in the role-play.

Unless . . . is there a boardroom in Haven as well? The possibility springs into my mind, but I file it away to wonder about later as he stops next to her beside the desk.

I'm failing at the dare, for the record. His stare takes on a life of his own, even as the scene plays out in front of me.

"You couldn't keep your fingers off your greedy little pussy while we were in front of people, could you?"

Her eyes stay downcast, but there's an obvious air of excitement buzzing around her as she squirms in her tall heels. *Is that how I looked when I stood there and the scene started?*

"Answer me, or I'll double your punishment."

She bites her lip. "No. I couldn't."

"You wanted to touch yourself where anyone could've seen you?"

"Yes," she whispers, but there's no shame in it, more like triumph. "You know I like—"

The man steps forward. "I know what you like, pet. And you're going to get your audience. Turn around and spread your legs."

Oh my God, they know we're watching them. The thought pops into my head, followed by, *Well, I would hope so.* Especially considering I wouldn't want to be watched without my knowledge.

Wait, I would want to be watched if I knew? I stiffen in the chair at the uncomfortable thought, but it takes a back seat when the woman follows his orders and he touches a hand to her lower back, then presses her chest down on the desk.

That was me before.

"Do you remember how it felt to have your tits pressed against the desk? How it felt to spread your legs as you waited for whatever I wanted to do to you?"

His voice deepens, taking on that raspy quality, making my nipples tighten into sensitive points as I shift in the chair, uncrossing my legs.

"Answer me."

"Yes. I remember."

"Good." The sound of a zipper hissing catches my attention, but it's not coming from the other couple.

Oh my God, is he . . .

"Your eyes just got so fucking big," my stranger says. "Are you wishing you could see my cock in my hand?"

My fingertips dig into the leather as I soak my panties.

"Spread your legs," he orders.

"But—"

"You're not in charge here, princess. Now, spread your legs."

The reminder demolishes any resistance, and I uncross my legs and inch them apart until my skirt is stretched to its limit.

The man in the office pulls off his tie and lowers it to the woman's back. "Roaming hands means that I'm going to have to tie them up so you can't break the rules anymore." He wraps the binding around her wrists and knots it together.

"You like that? Seeing her tied up?" my stranger asks from the corner.

I clear my throat to find my voice. "Yes." The admission produces another wave of moisture.

He groans, and I tear my eyes off the man checking the restraints to stare into the darkness again, wishing I could see *him*.

"Pull up your skirt. I want to see more."

I bite down on my lip at his order. His words are rougher now, and the tone evokes something in me that only he ever has. The urge to *let go and obey*.

I don't question. Don't hesitate. My fingers release their tight grip on the arms of the chair and pinch the hem of my dress.

"High. Show me everything."

I drag the fabric up my spread thighs until the lacy tops of my stockings appear. With every inch, I feel bolder.

"More."

I keep going and, finally, my black thong is visible.

"Look at them. Not me."

Cool air sweeps over my skin as I force my gaze to the window.

Why is it I couldn't take my eyes off the couple in the bedroom, and now I find an outline in the darkness even more magnetic than the erotic scene happening in front of me?

Because it's him.

The sound of skin smacking skin, followed by a woman's moan, forces my attention straight ahead.

Oh God. He's spanking her ass.

My stranger's comment from earlier—about how someone watching would have been able to see his handprint on my ass—slams into me. Who knew that a visual could be so hot?

"Touch yourself. I want to see your fingers buried in your panties."

My gaze jerks back to him.

"Don't watch me. Watch them, or you'll earn a punishment."

My hips rock back into the chair because I can't squeeze my legs together.

"Fuck, that turns you on even more than they do. You're a dirty little surprise. Now, move those fingers."

Like he controls my hand, I lift it from the arm of the chair and reach between my legs. I've never done this before. Never touched myself while someone watched. The closest I've ever come was when I nearly touched myself in the office before I knew I wasn't alone.

My fingertips hover over the lace.

"One . . ." His deep voice rings out. "Two . . ."

I know without asking that his count signals my punishment for hesitation.

When I slip my fingers behind the lace, he releases another groan.

"Fuck. You have no idea how goddamn sexy you are. With your skirt up, legs spread, and fingertips an inch from that tight cunt I haven't been able to get out of my mind. *Fuck me.*" He breathes the last two words like a prayer, and they embolden me.

Beneath my panties, I skate one fingertip down the seam of my lips, sliding effortlessly through the wetness gathered there.

I bite down on my lip, but a muffled moan sneaks out anyway. My lips part and my mouth drops open as I touch my clit.

"How wet are you?"

The scene in front of me blurs into a chorus of moans as a stronger wave of boldness seizes me. I pull my hand away and hold up my glistening fingertip.

"Soaked." My lips curve into a catlike smile.

His growl sends another flood of wetness between my legs.

"Naughty fucking girl. Suck it off. I want to know

how it tastes."

A rush of breath leaves my lips as my confidence falters.

"Now."

I raise my trembling fingers to my mouth and suck one clean of my own tart-sweet slickness.

"Tell me how it tastes."

The urgency underpinning his question spurs my boldness again.

"Why don't you come find out for yourself?"

CHAPTER 12

Temperance

WITH MY DARE, I'M TESTING BOUNDARIES. I can't help it. He's set off something inside me I can't control.

"I'm calling the shots here, princess. Lose the panties. I want to watch you finger yourself." His voice transforms into a deep growl.

Does that mean he's losing control? Do I want him to?

I stare into the darkness, debating.

No. I want him to be strong enough to take control from me and keep it.

"*Now.*"

The word comes out of the shadows like a growl, and I snap into action. I drag the black scrap of lace down my legs and kick it off my ankles.

"Throw them to me."

I reach down, pick up the fabric, and crumple

it into a ball before pitching it in his general direction. His hand comes out of the darkness to snag it in midair before bringing it toward his face.

"You smell fucking incredible, and I bet you taste even better. Get those fingers in your pussy. I want to watch you make yourself come."

How is it possible that watching the shadow of a man smell my underwear is hotter than whatever is happening in the next room? I've completely lost track of that because the man in this room is a million times more magnetic with his rough voice and filthy orders.

A rough voice and filthy orders that I'm quickly growing addicted to.

"You do not want to make me wait."

The warning rasps over my nipples, and I'm more aware than ever of my body and its completely obscene position. My fingers hover over the top of my right stocking, only inches away from my center.

Am I really going to do this?

The answer flashes through my brain without any hesitation.

Of course I am, but I'm going to make him want it just as bad as I do.

My hand drops to just above my pussy, and I dart out a fingertip to trace the path I've already taken.

I'm not just following orders—I'm putting on a show.

My finger circles my clit, and my eyes adjust

more to the darkness where he sits. His fist clenches tighter around my panties.

"I didn't say tease yourself."

"Too bad."

He moves quicker than I anticipated, rising out of the chair, shoving his cock back in his pants and buttoning them before crossing the room to stand directly in front of my spread legs. He crouches down and the unzipped fly of his pants gaps, allowing me a glimpse of his veined shaft.

"My eyes are up here."

My gaze cuts to his as he reaches out and grips the arms of the chair, boxing me in. The lace of my panties peeks out from beneath his flattened right hand.

"Don't stop on my account. We're just getting started." From his crouching position, he leans forward, dipping his face between my legs and inhaling deeply. "God, I want to taste you. Now, finger-fuck that pussy."

Speechless. He's rendered me completely speechless. However, my body doesn't suffer the same paralysis as my tongue.

My fingers grow a life of their own and slide between my legs. My gaze locks on his face and the hunger burning in those blue eyes.

Has anyone ever looked at me like that before? Like he might starve to death if he doesn't get a taste of me?

Power radiates through me and I'm spurred on, sliding deeper, spreading my pussy lips apart. Baring myself to his gaze.

It's indecent. Wanton. Dirty. *And I love it.*

"More."

I slide one finger inside and moan, letting my knees fall farther apart.

"Fuck. Yes."

My hips rock into my own little thrusts, and I fuck myself for him. My moans grow louder, and so do his growls.

He's coming unglued, but not faster than I am. My orgasm is sneaking up on me quicker than ever before in my life. Then again, I've never experienced anything nearly as incendiary as this moment.

"Make yourself come."

I wasn't waiting for his permission, but that order kicks up the urgency driving me to the next level.

When his nostrils flare, my vision begins to blur and I move my hand faster, pumping in and out and grinding the heel of my palm on my clit.

"I'm so close."

I pull my fingers free and press down hard on my clit, and my body responds like it's the button for my detonation.

CHAPTER 13

Temperance

A HOARSE SCREAM BREAKS FREE OF MY THROAT as my entire body tenses and my hips rock against the chair.

Calloused fingers pull my hand from between my legs, and he sucks my fingers into his mouth.

Oh my good God. That's the hottest thing I've ever seen.

After he licks them clean, he lets out a groan. "Tart, tangy, and oh-so-fucking smooth." He releases my fingers and rises, reaching out to wrap both hands around my waist. "You're about to get fucked so hard."

"God, yes."

I nod, but he's already lifting me off the chair like I don't weigh a thing and backing me up against a bare wall. As soon as he sets me on my feet, my spine pressed against it, he pulls a condom out of his pocket.

"Take my cock out."

My hands drop to his pants, releasing the button. The silk-lined fabric falls away as his dick springs free. He rolls the condom down his shaft and gives it a hard tug.

"You gonna be able to take it all? Because this is what you did. This is what you bought with your show. Your fucking sexy moans when you came. The taste of your sweet cunt."

"Yes." It comes out as a plea because I've never wanted anything more.

"Good."

He grips my waist again and lifts me up. "Wrap those legs around me."

My palms reach out to grip the solid slabs of his shoulders as I follow his order, lifting one leg to lock around his tattooed hip.

There's no way he can . . .

But he moves forward, lining up with my entrance, and his blue eyes pierce mine as he pushes inside me until he's buried to the hilt.

Like a live wire, raw energy charges between us. His nostrils flare as he squeezes me tighter, wraps my other leg around his hip, and pulls back before pounding into me.

This is what I've been dying for ever since I ran out of Haven like a scared little girl last weekend. His ownership, his dominance—and if I'm honest, his cock.

He plunges into me and withdraws, dragging over every sensitive nerve ending again and again.

He lifts me higher and keeps me aloft effortlessly in a stunning display of power. I buck against him, grinding my clit against his hard stomach as he stills.

When he pulls away again, I'm ready to beg.

"Please, I need to come."

He finally breaks my stare and glances toward the window into the office. "Look at them. Look at them right now."

I turn my head toward the window, and the man is fucking the woman bent over the desk, her hands bound behind her back.

Her mouth is open, like she's moaning her pleasure, but I can't hear anything over the roaring in my ears and the sound of my own heavy breathing.

"I want you to come for me. I want you to scream so loud, they can hear you through the soundproof walls."

My eyes cut back to him, and the other couple is already forgotten.

"Hold on."

I grip his shoulders as he carries me across the room to a couch and lowers me so my hips are tilted up on the arm. Once I'm settled, his thrusts begin again, hitting inside me at the perfect angle. I'm writhing, thrashing, moaning, and everything inside me threatens to break free when one of his hands slides between us to thumb my clit.

My scream pierces my own ears, but I don't care who hears me, because the pleasure barreling through me is more than I can process.

I'm splintering apart. Shattering.

He doesn't let me stop. The orgasm keeps going and so does he, pounding into me and unleashing another wave of overwhelming sensation. My voice turns hoarse, but I keep moaning like I'm some kind of wild creature, and maybe I am. This is what he does to me.

I'm completely under his control.

My body no longer belongs to me.

He owns it. Owns me.

I lose track of time, space, and every other damn thing as I embrace the intense pleasure surging through me until he finally lets loose a harsh roar and his cock pulses.

He pulls out and drops to his knees, his forehead resting on the arm of the couch between my legs, and one of his hands wraps around my calf.

I'm limp. Boneless. In this state, lying draped over a sofa with a man between my legs doesn't faze me in the least.

A wave of exhaustion hits me and my eyes flutter shut. I'm too tired to do anything but let go.

When I awaken, warmth surrounds me. I'm cocooned

in a soft, thick blanket, and there's a weight on my lap.

I blink a few times to adjust to the dim light of the room. I'm still in the library on the small sofa. The two-way mirror is dark, and there's a bottle of water, the expensive kind I would normally laugh at the thought of buying, resting against my stomach. Next to it, there's a note.

That's all I need to see to know he's gone.

Didn't want to leave you alone, but I had to go.
I want to see you again.

The fact that he left doesn't bother me. Instead, I'm filled with warmth, and it's not solely because of the fluffy blanket tucked around me.

He wants to see me again.

Why does it feel so good to know that?

Do I want to see him?

As soon as the question forms in my mind, the answer is clear.

Yes. Definitely.

I uncurl from my cocoon and rise on shaky legs, using a hand on the back of the sofa to steady myself. A small smile curves my lips when I realize my dress and stockings have been restored to their rightful place, and my shoes are waiting next to my purse.

As I slide them on, my brain latches on to one thing that's missing from the room other than my stranger.

My panties.

I press my lips together to stifle a giggle.

Kinky son of a bitch. I have no idea why I like that so much, but I do.

As I make my way down to the valet and then drive the long miles home to downtown and my apartment, I can't help but relive the encounter over and over.

When I finally slide into my own bed, my body feeling deliciously used, I question my sanity.

I don't know anything about him except he's dangerous. At least, according to Magnolia.

But even that doesn't curb my growing addiction.

My rational brain tells me I can't keep doing this. That tonight has to be the last time. It's not smart. It's not safe. But my body disagrees.

I have to keep doing this.

But there's one massive hurdle—I have no way to get in touch with him.

Some of the fluttery feeling in my belly fades away.

What if he doesn't find me?

He will. He has to feel this too.

I fall asleep with a smile on my face.

CHAPTER 14

Temperance

THE NEXT MORNING, AS I LOCK MY BRONCO IN the parking lot of Seven Sinners, my mind is still on the tangled sheets of my bed and the filthy dreams that had me waking up sweaty and begging. Every twinge of my sore muscles keeps last night firmly fixed in my mind.

I'm addicted to this stranger, and I don't even care how crazy it is.

Those thoughts evaporate like water on a blazing-hot tin roof when the yelling starts.

"How dare you pass off some piece of trash as my art!"

Gregor Standish's insult slams into my belly like a sucker punch as he slams the door of a Range Rover. He storms toward me, his face mottled and red.

"Mr. Standish—"

"Did you see this garbage?" He waves a

newspaper in my direction as he advances.

Stepping away from the flapping pages, I clear my throat. "Sir, if you'll please—"

"They put *my name* under the picture of that abomination. I'm going to be the laughingstock of the art community by lunchtime."

"Sir, please—"

"I can't have my name associated with that tasteless pedestrian refuse masquerading as art!"

Each word scores a direct hit, reinforcing what I've always feared—my work isn't good enough to be seen. The burn of tears stings the back of my eyes. The death of a dream is never painless, even if it's an arrogant asshole wielding the executioner's ax.

I straighten my spine, determined not to allow him to see how deadly his strikes are. He can never know that the piece was mine. No one can.

"That's quite enough, Mr. Standish. If you have a complaint to lodge, you can do it civilly or I'll have to ask you to leave." I inject authority into my tone, even though I'm crumpling on the inside. Shoring up my defenses now is too little, too late, but I have no choice but to pretend.

Standish's face turns an even darker shade of red, and if he wasn't such a jerk, I might worry about his blood pressure. As it stands, I can't find it in me to give a damn about his health. Not when he's eviscerating me.

"My artwork—my *actual* art—is inside, and if

you try to keep me from it, I will take everything from this company and that bitch who runs it."

As soon as he insults Keira, steel lodges in my spine and I level a hard stare in his direction. "Mr. Standish, it would be in your best interest to stop right there." He opens his mouth to spill more vitriol, but I keep speaking, a new confidence in my tone. After all, it's much easier to stand up for her than for myself. "You will not like the consequences of your actions if you don't."

The expression on his face turns snide. "Don't you tell me what to do. You don't understand who you're dealing with."

It's on the tip of my tongue to tell him that he's the one who doesn't have a clue who he's dealing with, and any further comments are going to mean that he ends his day in a body bag, but I don't. This man will not be calmed with reason or threats. He's completely unhinged.

"I looked you up when you wouldn't answer my calls. No wonder you're so completely inept at this job. COO? You're still a glorified secretary." His glare turns gleefully cruel. "I don't know why I was surprised. You're just swamp trash, which is exactly what that sculpture looked like. So you tell whoever made that piece of garbage that I'm coming after them too for trying to pass it off as mine."

Direct. Hit.

Instead of staggering backward and letting him

know he's scored a painful point, I square my shoulders. "The mistake was innocent, Mr. Standish, and might I point out, *sir*, that it wouldn't have happened if you had allowed us to move your piece, or if you had actually shown up on time, per the instructions I provided you."

He wrinkles his nose like someone just waved a hunk of rotten gator meat under it. "You should've waited. Just one more example of your mismanagement. This was no innocent mistake. This was planned."

As much as I want to shout at him and tell him it's not in any way, shape, or form *my* fault, and he couldn't be more wrong about every single one of his conclusions, I know that screaming in the parking lot isn't going to be helpful or productive.

I'd much prefer to shoot him in the parking lot, but prison orange isn't exactly my color.

My brother would get rid of the body, though . . . The unvarnished thought puts a bloodthirsty smile on my face.

"I'm not going to argue with you any longer, Mr. Standish. Please accept my apologies, and maybe we can both agree that Mary's House still received a substantial benefit from the auction last night, even with the mistake. Therefore, the purpose was still served and you get to keep your piece, perhaps to donate for an even larger benefit to a charitable organization in the future."

I'm congratulating myself on sounding poised and professional, when what I really want to tell him is if Mount doesn't kill him for what he said about Keira, someone else surely will for being such a nasty human being.

Standish's face screws into an evil expression as he darts forward, wrapping his fingers hard around my upper arm, his fingers digging into my skin. "Only someone so plebeian would ever think something so simplistic."

I yank my arm free, and his nails scrape my skin.

"Do we have a problem here?"

The door slams behind Louis Artesian, the head of distilling operations, as he comes toward us.

"Yes, we have a goddamn problem," Standish says, his lips curling.

Louis looks to me, concern edging his tone. "Do you need me to call security?"

I meet his kind brown eyes before looking pointedly at Gregor Standish. "That's up to Mr. Standish. If he wants to collect his artwork, he'll need to contain himself."

"How dare you, you—"

My phone rings, interrupting whatever insult he's planning to throw at me next. I pull it out of my bag and look down at the screen. *Keira.*

"Excuse me, Mr. Standish. I'll speak with Ms. Kilgore about your concerns. If you're able to calm down, perhaps you'll be allowed inside the building to collect your art."

I walk away from him as he sputters at Louis, but I don't look back as I answer my phone. "Good morning, boss."

"What's going on?"

I unlock the back door, open it, and make sure to lock it behind me. "Standish is having a meltdown in the parking lot. Making accusations and threats. I tried to explain, but he's not listening."

"Of course not. And I'm also not that surprised because I just read the one-star review he left for Seven Sinners on every single online platform in the known universe. V and I are almost there. He'll take care of him."

In Keira's world, *taking care of someone* means something different than it does to most people.

I open my mouth to ask if she's sure that's necessary, but Keira has already ended the call.

This is *not* how I expected my day to go.

CHAPTER 15

Temperance

THANKFULLY, I DON'T HAVE TO FACE STANDISH again, and I try to get to work and attempt to forget about how V might be *taking care of him.* I'm only marginally successful when my phone rings after lunch.

"Hi, Temperance, Valentina Hendrix. I'm hoping you can help me out."

Please don't let it be about the sculpture, I beg the universe. After Standish's brutal verbal attack this morning, my guts feel like they've been through a meat grinder, and I don't have the emotional distance to talk about it objectively right now.

Still, I keep the positivity in my tone just like a good COO would. "I'm happy to help if I'm able. What can I do for you, ma'am?"

"Valentina, please. And I'm pretty sure you already know what I want. The name of the artist, since

I wasn't able to buy the sculpture last night from the winner." She pauses and I consider how to respond, but I'm not quick enough. "If you have the person's name, you'd be doing him or her a great disservice by not passing along some information."

"What kind of information?"

"The kind that could be very lucrative."

"I'm afraid I—"

"Just hear me out before you say anything."

I go silent.

"I don't know if you're aware, but I love to feature local artists at Noble Art, and I have a gut feeling that it was a local who made that sculpture. There was too much passion in that piece for it not to be made by someone who has the blood of this city running through their veins."

I say nothing, hoping my silence will help her get to the point faster. It works.

"I want to purchase, rather than consign, a few more pieces with the same feel, and I'm willing to pay a fair price for them because I know I'll be able to make money. I have several clients who will snap them up as quickly as I can get them into the gallery."

The confidence in her tone is a balm to some of the wounds Standish inflicted, but I'm not ready to give her any kind of answer except . . .

"If I can get in touch, I'll pass the information on. I can't make any promises, though."

"There's no time limit on the offer," she says, and

I relax a fraction, even though I can hear the victory in her tone. "But . . . I'll be honest, with the publicity from the auction and the rising interest and speculation, now is the time to strike. So, if this person has any kind of business sense at all, it would be extremely intelligent for him or her to get in touch with me sooner rather than later."

My business sense is something I pride myself on, so her comment feels like a dare.

"I'll make sure to add that."

"I know most artists aren't the best business people, but the ones that are . . . you'd be surprised how solid of a living they can make in this town if they play their cards right. It's not as difficult as you'd think, especially if the person is smart about it. Feel free to pass that along as well."

The hair on the back of my neck goes up like a dog scenting trouble. *Does she suspect?* The hints she's dropping seem specifically delivered to pique my curiosity, but all the ugliness from Standish still remains, casting a pall over the entire situation.

"I'll pass it along, but I can't make any promises I'll be able to get you a response." I work to keep all emotion out of my voice, which takes some effort.

"Thank you, Temperance. I appreciate it. Let me give you the best ways to contact me."

I write down both of Valentina's numbers and her email address, then hang up the phone, wondering what the hell I'm supposed to do with that information.

One statement continues to play on repeat through my brain. "*You'd be surprised how solid of a living they can make . . .*"

It doesn't matter, I tell myself. Art will never provide the same stability as a regular paycheck coming from Seven Sinners. And even more than that, welding scrap metal together and calling it art will never provide the kind of respectability I want, especially within the art community. I've worked too long and too hard to get where I am to even consider throwing it away to chase some crazy dream.

But one piece sold for fifty thousand dollars, a voice in my head whispers.

"Yeah, because someone else's name was attached to it. Someone people had actually heard of and care about."

I feel every inch the fraud because of it. None of those paddles would have gone up in the air if the bidders had known that the person who'd picked through the scrap yard and spent hours designing and welding was *me*.

I'm a nobody. But at least I'm making a name for myself here.

And besides, I'm already taking enough risks right now.

CHAPTER 16

Temperance

B Y THE TIME I FIND A PARKING SPOT IN THE Quarter, two blocks away from my apartment, the weight of the day has me dragging ass to my gate that reminds me altogether too much of the wrought iron marking the entrance to Haven. It seems like everything reminds me of it today, or maybe I just don't want to forget last night.

It's already nearly seven when I unlock the gate and carry my bag down the narrow brick pathway leading into the enclosed courtyard out back. Music from Harriet's open window—opera, of course— greets me as I stop and survey what looks like a party in the making.

"Tempe, girl, that you?" Harriet calls from the outdoor table where a lavish buffet is set up under a huge live oak draped with thick blankets of Spanish moss and resurrection fern. Fairy lights and solar-powered Chinese lanterns dangle from the branches, and the tinkle of the fountains and the koi pond are the only sounds beyond the noise of the city and the music. The blue water of the small splash pool reflects the lights, adding ambience.

I jerk my head, looking around for the other guests, worried I'm interrupting, but no one else is here. At least, not yet.

"Are you having a party?"

Interacting with humans tonight, beyond my landlady, might be more than I can handle.

She lifts her champagne flute with a shake of her head. "Party? No. Not tonight. Come join me."

The decadent setup of the table would seem extravagant for one person by anyone else's standards, but one thing Harriet believes in is embracing life and enjoying every moment. Calling for a takeaway spread like this for herself shouldn't surprise me at all.

She's the one person who I might actually be able to spill my entire story to and get real, valid advice on the situation Valentina has presented me with. Harriet's a shrewd businesswoman who owns a few shops in the Quarter, but doesn't run any of them herself. Instead, she spends her time painting and traveling the world.

"You have another wineglass?"

Tilting her head back, she laughs. "Silly question." She produces one from behind the centerpiece on the table and reaches for a bottle of champagne resting on ice. A knot of tension in my upper back loosens a few degrees. She pours, almost letting it overflow, before handing it off to me as I approach.

As she raises her glass to clink the rim of mine, she says, "Champagne is the answer tonight. I don't care what the question is. You can write that down if you'd like. Feel free to refer to it whenever you look like you're carrying the weight of the world on your shoulders like you do now. You need to get laid more often, girl."

I choke on the perfectly crisp, bubbly liquid and lower the glass as I cough. "Thanks for the tip."

"You need more than the tip. You need a guy who knows what the hell he's doing. Preferably by multiple guys so you can compare styles. But not at the same time." She grins at me with a wink. "Unless you're into that sort of thing."

"Umm . . . I'll get right on that . . ." I trail off and realize I probably should have chosen my words with more care.

"You're damn right you will. Find a man and climb on top to ride."

I'm tempted to drain this glass, but out of respect for the pricey label on the bottle, I take a sip instead.

"This is delicious, by the way." At this point, I'm ready to change the subject to just about anything.

"Of course it is. I don't swill from the twist-off bottles. I'm not sixty anymore."

Harriet's comment scares up a chuckle from my throat. She's truly one of my most favorite people in the world.

"You're sure there's no special occasion we're celebrating tonight with this fancy spread?" I ask the question more to make conversation than anything else.

"It's . . ." She looks at me, her brow wrinkled. "What day of the week is it?"

"Friday."

She gestures with her glass. "It's finally Friday! Or Fri-*yay*, as I like to call it. Isn't that all the reason we need? Not that one needs a reason to celebrate still kicking around on this spinning bit of rock hurtling through the universe."

"Fair enough." I lift the glass to my lips again and sip, letting the crisp wine smooth some of the battered edges of my soul.

It's not usually my MO to take solace in alcohol, but tonight . . . tonight I'm not sure I care. It's not like I'm drinking whiskey, the devil that dragged my dad under. Seven Sinners was his label of choice when he had the money, which he rarely did.

Makes my job kind of ironic, doesn't it?

Harriet picks up a bone china plate emblazoned with skulls and flowers and loads it with delicacies.

"Here, try this aged cheddar. It's decadent. And these grapes taste like they came straight off the vine. Speaking of vines, I bought a vineyard this morning."

My chin jerks in her direction. "What? Where?"

She hands me the plate. "Italy, of course. Where else would I buy a vineyard?"

I lower the selection of meats, cheeses, and fruits to the table and absently reach for a linen napkin while I turn her statement over in my head. "Have you been planning the acquisition long?"

Harriet's throaty laugh washes over me, instantly making me realize how silly the question probably is.

"Of course not. A friend of mine mentioned today he was tight on money and was going to sell to his neighbor—a boor of a man who insulted my landscapes by calling them *quaint* while I was there—so I offered to buy it purely out of spite. He's wanted the land for years, but Pietro has managed to hold on to it, even though he has a terrible head for business. He's much better at cunnilingus."

I choke on the piece of cheese I just popped into my mouth.

"Good Lord, girl. Do you need the Heimlich?" Harriet pronounces the word like she's suddenly become a native German speaker. Which, for all I know, she could be. Nothing about this woman surprises me anymore, except, apparently, her dropping the word *cunnilingus* over champagne.

I cover my mouth as I cough and shake my head. "That's . . . interesting."

"It really is. He has this technique that's truly unique. He does this thing with his tongue that . . . I don't know how to explain it."

She glances up at the sky as though trying to find the right words, and I change the subject as quickly as humanly possible, latching on to anything I can.

"How do you handle that?"

"Well, normally I'd grab him by the hair, but those patches around the side are getting a bit sparse—"

Thankful I'm not chewing anymore or in danger of choking, I quickly interrupt. "No, I mean the comments about your art."

"From small-minded idiots? Usually, I pay them no mind." She smiles sweetly. "But sometimes I like to ruin their lives. It depends on my mood. This one time, I contacted a hit man . . ." She looks away as though remembering the incident, and I'm a little frightened by what she might say next.

There's no doubt in my mind that Harriet is batshit crazy, but I'm also a little in awe of her.

"You had someone killed?"

Her expression sharpens. "Darling, don't you know you never admit to those things? Legal Basics 101." She reaches for her plate and loads it again. "Why the sudden interest in the irrelevant opinions of others? Your *friend* finally going to get over herself and sell one of those sculptures?"

This time, I nearly choke on a piece of meat.

Harriet's been after me to sell one of the two pieces in my apartment. My furniture may not be much to write home about, but she's enraptured with the small sculpture of a blue heron, my mama's favorite bird. I'm not sure why I keep it around, but I can't bring myself to sell it either.

I take a solid ten seconds to decide whether to seek her advice, but it's already a foregone conclusion. Harriet's opinion, even though it may be zany, is one that I value.

"She actually did. It was an accident."

Harriet's smile threatens to crack her face. "I knew it! I saw the paper this morning while I was having my beignet. There's no way that douchebag Standish could've made that piece. I recognized the style immediately. Shows how low that jackass would stoop to try to take credit for it."

Her assessment of the situation stuns me. "Actually, he was furious to have it attributed to him. Said it was trash."

The admission feels like glass shards slicing up my throat.

Harriet's smile fades. "If there was a vineyard he wanted to buy, I'd buy it up this instant. The man is a disgrace to the community. He called me a crazy old lady just last week when I asked him how he found so many crayons to melt to make his latest blob. God forbid he ever makes something brown. It'll look like he's been eating too much dairy and decided to put his excrement to use."

The laughter that bubbles up deep in my belly is the second-best balm to my shredded soul, following

Harriet's ruthless assessment and accompanying cackle.

When we both stop to catch our breath and clutch our stomachs, her expression shifts to sobriety for a beat.

"Normally I wouldn't be so harsh about art. It's all subjective, after all, but I truly can't abide that man."

It's on the tip of my tongue to say *after his comments about Keira, you might not have to abide him much longer*, but I keep it in following Harriet's Legal Basics 101 comment.

"Well, his subjective opinion was pretty brutal."

She waves it off. "I would say that the fifty Gs it netted speaks for itself."

The conversation I had with Valentina pushes to the forefront of my mind. "A gallery owner made an inquiry about more pieces. She wants to purchase them outright rather than take them on consignment."

Harriet's pale eyebrows rise. "Is that so? I'd say that counts a hell of a lot more than Standish's opinion, not that her art requires monetary validation, but cold hard cash is always nice. Is she going to do it?"

I study the bubbles rising in my champagne flute. "I don't know."

Harriet's long silence drags my attention back to her face. "Do you know what would be the height of stupidity?"

"What?"

"To not take every opportunity to do the thing that makes your soul the happiest, especially when someone's willing to pay you for it."

Her easily dispensed wisdom and the knowledge in her faded blue eyes hit me like a fist to the gut.

"You should pass that along to your friend. Free of charge." She winks.

"But what if . . . what if she hasn't created anything new in a very long time? What if she's not sure she still can? What if she lacks time because she has a real job to pay the bills?"

Harriet sips her champagne. "Excuses are like assholes. Everyone's got one."

I laugh quietly, shaking my head. "I suppose they are."

She gestures to the sunset fading in the sky. "There are twenty-four usable hours in every day, especially if you know how to get the good drugs." Her lips quirk into a smile before she turns more serious. "But all joking aside, it all comes down to one question. How bad does she want it, and how hard is she willing to chase that dream? If she's not willing to make sacrifices, especially a sacrifice of something as simple and easy as sleep, then she doesn't want it bad enough."

How bad do I want it?

Isn't that what it always comes down to? My entire life has been a struggle, sometimes with me fighting tooth and nail to have the opportunity to go after what I want. A college degree. A job at Seven Sinners. Respectability.

No one has handed me a damn thing. And now, for the first time, someone is holding out one of my dreams on a silver platter, and I'm questioning whether to reach out with both hands and grab on?

That's not like me at all. In fact, I'm not sure I even recognize myself through this haze of indecision.

"Let me know when you're going to finally admit there's no friend in this equation so we can start talking about what *you're* going to do about this. If you won't take ownership of your dream, you're never going to achieve it."

I stand and round the table to refill my champagne flute while I digest Harriet's words. They don't surprise me. She's uncannily perceptive. I take another sip and set the glass down on the table, dropping any hint of pretense.

"Standish called it trash. An abomination." Uttering the words tears open the wounds he inflicted and splays my true reservations wide.

"Standish wouldn't know talent if it slapped him in the face. He's too busy inspecting his own anal cavity." Harriet reaches out to take my hand in her small, wrinkled one. "But, darling, if you're going to do this, you're going to need to grow a much thicker skin. There will always be critics. Doubters. Haters. If there weren't, then you wouldn't be doing it right. In the immortal words of Tay-Tay, you have to shake it off."

Releasing my hand, she waves me off. "Now, go change your clothes, track down a welder and some scrap metal, and *create*. Here's your sign, girl. It's time."

CHAPTER 17

Temperance

It's not quite as simple as going to find a welder and scrap metal, like Harriet said. Or maybe it is. I guide my Bronco the next morning down a road I know by heart. A road I've wished a million times I could forget.

The road that leads home.

For others, going home brings feelings of nostalgia, warmth, and maybe excitement, but for me it's more complicated. Especially because I don't have a home anymore. The falling-down old cabin has probably been reclaimed by the swamp by now after being left in disrepair for so long. Either way, I'm stopping before I get to the dirt track that would take me back to the place where I lived most of my life.

Buckshot holes puncture a rusted yellow sign showing a black arrow. My designation is just around the next sharp curve.

There's another reason it's not as simple as going to find a welder and scrap metal. Coming here to create also involves asking for favors, something I've never been good at, and facing some painful, bitter memories.

Should I have called first?

It's not like I could truly forget the number, even though I've long since deleted it. Then again, it's not like Elijah Devereux has probably started answering his phone on the regular. Some things never change.

Gravel crunches under my Bronco's tires as I brake and make the right-hand turn down the dirt road that leads me to a chain-link fence topped with barbed wire. Moss blankets the old NO TRESPASSING signs, but Elijah has added a few new ones.

WE DON'T CALL 911. Beneath the metal sign hangs an old AK-47.

Classy, Eli. Also, very truthful. Out here, people don't trust the police as much as they trust their own guns and ammo.

Authority is always met with suspicion, and it's much easier to get rid of a body in the swamp than to explain to the sheriff what happened after the fact.

The gators in these parts are well fed, and not just by fish.

Shockingly, the chain-link fence is partially open. Though, I suppose it is early on a Saturday morning, which means that folks around here are working on their cars and might need parts from the local scrap yard.

Devereux Recycling, formerly Devereux Junk, is where I welded that piece that sold for fifty thousand dollars.

Looking at the rows of cars with busted windshields and flat tires, it's hard to believe this place is even worth that much. But it is. Elijah has made damn sure of it.

I drive through the fence and note the dogs in the kennel alongside the trailer where, if things haven't changed that much, Elijah still lives. The lights in the trailer are off, but that doesn't mean anything. He could be anywhere. Elijah doesn't exactly follow the rules of polite society, including when one should sleep versus be awake.

The dogs stand at attention, salivating as they watch me drive by, and there's no way in hell I'd want to face one of them out in the open. I doubt they remember me, if they're even the same pair of Cane Corsos I remember from a few years back. Mean as hell, but twice as loyal.

Once upon a time, the dogs that ran free through here at night listened to me when I gave orders. But I'm not that girl anymore, even though a sense of belonging grips me as I drive farther.

The rays of the brilliant sunrise glint off the partially stripped cars for as far as the eye can see as I maneuver my Bronco toward the big multicolored metal building about a hundred yards away.

Strangely enough, I'm still more comfortable in scrap yards and around chopped cars than I am at charity events toasting with champagne. It's the hard truth I've been trying to whitewash from my life, but I guess your soul always knows where it comes from.

I'm definitely tripping a few different early-warning systems as I drive through, even though it seems like this place is deserted.

Elijah is too paranoid not to know everything that's happening on his property at any given time. He also doesn't care if people call him a conspiracy theorist or a crazy motherfucker. Basically, he's never given a single damn what people think of him. Something I wish I've been able to embrace.

Instead, for me, I equate people liking me with caring about me. And if they don't care about me, somehow that makes me worthless. I've had enough feelings of worthlessness drilled into my psyche for years that I'm not sure I'll ever shake it.

And all of that worthlessness comes from out here, where the scent of decay is more homey than apple pie.

Finally, I reach the metal building and find the massive overhead doors are down, but that doesn't mean a whole lot either. I park my Bronco and throw the emergency brake. I'm not sure why, but if he gets it into his head to try to tow my car out of here, it'll at least make it a touch more difficult. Not much, considering how good Elijah is with a slim jim, but it's something.

This is the kind of people I come from. The kind who can steal a car in less than sixty seconds, and with fewer incidents than in that Nicolas Cage movie.

I wait for a few minutes, wondering if the door will open or someone is going to come out with a shotgun, but it doesn't happen.

Elijah must be up and about, at least I assume, based on the faint whiff of hot metal in the air. I shut the door quietly and practically tiptoe to the overhang of the building before gripping the silver handle and easing the door open.

He's waiting for me with an angle grinder in his right hand. "And here I'd given up hope on you ever showing your face here again."

"How'd you know it was me?"

"I got more cameras than Fort Knox, but your exhaust gave you away first. You've still got a leak." He shoves his safety glasses up into his sandy-blond hair. "Should've let me fix it when I offered."

"I was—"

"Too busy. I remember. You're too busy for a lot of things, Tempe. Including anyone that doesn't fit with your new life."

The stab of guilt slices clean through me like my brother's buck knife through a gator's hide, but I cover it with defensiveness.

"Excuse me for trying to make something of myself."

His navy gaze turns dark, almost black. "I thought you already were something, but I guess I was wrong."

Another stab.

I knew this was going to be hard, but I didn't expect to once again have to armor myself for battle. "I didn't come here to argue, Eli."

"Then what the hell did you come for?"

"I want to work."

His brows go up, and he sets the angle grinder on the partially chopped car. "Never thought I'd see the day. Thought you were too good for that stuff now that you're living in the Quarter and drinking that fancy whiskey."

"I don't drink whiskey," I snap back.

"I remember one night that you did."

He tilts his head to the side, and the memory assails me. Elijah and me in the backseat of a car . . . the night I lost my virginity.

"That was the last time."

He grins. "I got a bigger backseat these days. You're always welcome."

"I'll pass. Now, are you going to let me work?"

He looks me up and down, taking in every inch of the jeans I barely have time to wear anymore, and the old LSU T-shirt that I have tied up in back.

"Help me finish up this car, and the welder and workshop are all yours for as long as you need them."

My mouth drops open. "I'm not committing a

frigging felony today."

"Damn, you've got that self-righteous act down. Wouldn't be the first time. Remember how you helped me boost that car the night we fucked in the backseat?"

"I was young and stupid. Clearly."

"Well, you don't seem to have wised up all that much if you're back here asking me for favors. Seems like you've decided to go slummin'."

I want to punch him in the face, but I don't do stuff like that anymore. My misspent youth is long over, and I'm respectable now.

I spin on the heel of my scarred work boot, intending to march my ass right back to my Bronco. I don't need this. I can find somewhere else to—

"Aw, come on, Tempe. You can't even take a little ribbin' anymore. When'd you go get all delicate? That ain't the girl I knew."

"I've *changed*."

He grabs the angle grinder and fires it up again. "Guess we'll see how much." He flips down his safety glasses.

I'm two steps from the door when he says something that stops me cold.

"The girl I knew wasn't a quitter either."

CHAPTER 18

Temperance

I TURN AND FACE ELIJAH, ANGER BOILING MY blood.

"I'm not a quitter."

"Sure looks like it. You quit on everyone else in your life except that fancy job of yours. I'm surprised you troubled yourself to come all the way out here, and now you're just gonna walk away because you can't stand to get your hands dirty anymore."

I fist those very hands he refers to on my hips. "I'm not afraid of anything, especially not of getting my hands dirty. And certainly not of you."

He jerks his chin. "Then get your ass over here and put on some safety glasses. We got a car to chop, and then you've got some shit to weld."

My teeth threaten to crack with how hard I'm clenching my jaw.

I don't like being told what to do. I don't like

being told who I am and who I'm not. And I really don't like backing down from a challenge.

That's how I ended up stealing that first car and ending up in the backseat. My brother threatened to beat me black and blue when he found out, but it didn't stop me.

No. It took something a hell of a lot more than that.

I square my shoulders and cross the stained concrete floor, my heavy boots pounding as hard as the vein in my forehead.

I whip a pair of safety glasses off the nearest workbench and put them on, not caring if they're clean. I shed the perfectionist part of my persona when I drove away from downtown and returned to my past.

Here, I'm not worried about trying to fit in or what someone's going to think if they see the facade I've built slip. They've already seen the real me anyway.

"Give me a grinder. Let's get this shit done."

Once I have the tool in hand, I get to work. I don't need instructions on where the VINs are that need to be ground off, or where we need to cut. As the saying goes, this ain't my first rodeo.

Working together with the only sound in the building coming from metal on metal, we finish in record time.

When Elijah finally turns his tool off and steps away, I do the same. He tosses me a rag.

"Good to see you haven't lost your touch."

"You're going to let me use the workshop, your metal, and your tools as much as I need, and you're not going to give me any shit about it."

He crosses his arms and leans against the workbench behind him. "Is that right?"

"Yeah."

"And what are you gonna give me in return?"

"Not a damn thing."

His chest heaves with laughter. "Funny. You know that ain't how shit works around here."

He's right, but I'm not about to offer what I know he would prefer to take as payment in a heartbeat—me.

"It's called paying it forward, Devereux. Good karma." I mimic his posture and cross my arms, leaning back on my heels.

"That sounds like some hipster bullshit to me. You want to use my shit, you pay for it."

"How much?" I ask.

He shakes his head, a sly smile curving his lips. "I don't want your money, girl. You know that."

"Well, you're sure as hell not getting anything else from me."

He uncrosses his arms and walks toward me, his eyes narrowing as he scrutinizes my face. His boots halt only a few inches from mine.

"You got yourself a man these days? Is that the issue?"

I think of the man who has been haunting my thoughts for the last week. "Maybe."

This time, Elijah's forehead creases with shock. "Oh yeah? Who's the lucky son of a bitch?"

"You wouldn't know him." It's basically the only answer I can give without admitting that I don't know him either. At least, nothing beyond the wild addiction I've developed.

"I know a lot more people than you think. What's his name?"

A bolt of shame shoots through me at the reminder that I don't know that either. "Doesn't matter."

Elijah steps back, and I'm not sure what does it, but he relents on the subject. "Then you're gonna bring me a case of whiskey every time you come."

"Fine—" I start to agree to what is a simple request, but he keeps speaking.

"And you're gonna owe me a favor. Consider it payin' it forward," he says with a wink.

A favor isn't something I want to owe Elijah, but it's the quickest way to get what I want.

"Fine, but it has limits."

He shrugs. "We'll see about that. Now, go make something. Show me you haven't totally buried your magic under a pile of boring paperwork."

I've lost track of time, but I know hours have passed. When I step back and survey my work, my lips stretch in a smile. It's a phoenix rising out of the flames, and it's incredible.

I've still got it.

I tug the shop rag out of my back pocket and swipe it over my forehead to catch the dripping sweat my worn bandana didn't.

My arms and shoulders are sore from cutting, hammering, and welding, but it was worth it. Even the scrapes on my arms that my gloves didn't prevent are badges of honor. A sense of accomplishment floods my system, along with pride and satisfaction.

It took coming back here and seeing it through new eyes to realize I don't care what some stuck-up old asshole like Standish says. My art is not junk.

It's revitalization in the most basic way. Taking the old and unwanted, and refashioning it into something new and beautiful that will make people stop and stare.

The copper flames—hammered pieces of tubing and wire, torched to take on a red patina—look like they're actually burning brightly beneath and alongside the bird.

To create it, I used car parts. Plumbing components. Pieces ripped off of old appliances. It was a mad dash through the scrap and recycling yard, grabbing anything that looked promising, a wild process of piecing together the vision in my head, and a flat-out sprint to bring it to life.

But I did it.

I really did it.

"Well, fuck me, that's cool as shit," Elijah says from the garage door, which I heaved open in an attempt to stop myself from shedding a few more gallons of sweat.

I yank the bandana off my head and swipe it over my forehead. "Thanks."

He closes the distance between us. "I didn't think you had it in you anymore. Proved me wrong."

I shift my gaze in his direction without moving my head. "Does that mean you're going to drop your conditions on me using your space?"

He snorts a laugh. "Not a fucking chance. You pay to play here. That's life, girl. Should know that by now."

My stomach gnaws at my backbone and releases a loud growl.

"You want to grab something to eat?" Elijah says. "Crawfish boil already started at Rickety. Bet a few people would love to see you."

By Rickety, he means the Rickety Shack, one of the only restaurants within ten miles and a staple in these parts. The crawfish boil is a Saturday-night tradition. And me going with Elijah would send the wrong message on every level.

I'm not going backward in life, only forward.

"Sorry. Can't. I'm busy." I pull off my grimy gloves

and look down at my hands. I'm impressed with the limited number of cuts, scrapes, and broken nails. Totally worth it. Now I just have to clean myself up and decide what I'm busy doing tonight so I don't feel like I just lied.

Elijah's voice turns hard. "Hot date with a guy who expects you to be some perfect little princess?"

I wish, is the first thought in my head, but I don't voice it. My stranger hasn't surfaced again, even though I've kept my eyes open, expecting to see either him or one of those magic little cards, but I've been totally SOL on both counts. Every day that passes has me thinking about it more. The craving keeps growing stronger. But that's not something I'm going to say to Elijah.

"None of your business."

"Bet I could do you better." He knows me well enough to taunt effectively.

I shoot him a killing look. "Doubtful."

Elijah crosses his arms over his chest and instead of being cowed, he postures. "Is that so? You think you're the only one who's changed over the years, Tempe? You think no one else has learned a damn thing new or moved out of the little box where you want to keep everyone in your past?"

I'm not going to give him the satisfaction of arguing. "Are you going to help me load this into my Bronco or what?"

Elijah glances back to the phoenix. "Maybe I

want to keep it. Use it as yard art."

My gaze snaps to his. "Someone paid fifty grand for one of my sculptures in the last week, and you think I'm going to let you keep it as yard art? Not a chance."

"Whoa-ho-ho. There she is. There's the fire and sass you've been hiding beneath that prim attitude. Fake attitude, I might add. Does your man know the real you, Temperance? Or does he just know the perfect little shell you show the rest of the world?"

"He knows how it feels to have me coming hard on his dick, so I'm pretty sure that's all that matters."

As soon as the bold words are out, I know I've made a mistake. I'm not going back down that road with Elijah, no matter how easy it would be. Time to get out of here, because this place is wearing off on me.

Elijah stalks forward until we're practically nose to nose. "So do I. Maybe he and I could compare notes."

CHAPTER 19

Temperance

I FLIP FROM RADIO STATION TO RADIO STATION ON my way home, but every damn song sets me on edge, making me want something I can't have.

Him.

I never realized exactly how frustrating this could be. It's not that wanting what I can't have is new to me—because it certainly isn't. But normally I'm able to bury the craving deep beneath all the other feelings I don't want to face.

I'm failing this time.

Going home to spend Saturday night by myself just won't do tonight, but going out to a bar by myself doesn't sound like fun either.

This is when it'd be nice to have friends. But working all the time makes having friends inconvenient at best and impossible at worst.

I pull into a parking spot a block away from my

apartment, and pick my way down the broken concrete sidewalk to the gate that once again reminds me of the club and the man I've got to stop thinking about.

When the metal clangs shut behind me, Harriet's voice comes from the base of the curved wrought iron staircase just outside her back door that leads up to my apartment.

"Oh good. You saved me from having to climb those awful stairs. I was just about to leave you a note."

"What's going on?"

She's wearing a peach feather boa and a jaunty hat in the same color sits on her curls.

"Taking a last-minute trip with a gentleman friend. I'm past due for renewing my membership in the mile-high club." Her statement is so matter of fact, that I can't help but choke on my laugh.

"Where are you headed?"

"Norway, I think. Or maybe he said Nicaragua. It could've been Naples. Regardless, it'll be a good time. I'll be back in a few weeks. Maybe a month. We'll see how long he can entertain me." She bustles over to hug me, and the feather boa tickles my nose. "Take care of yourself, dear. Get some dick."

I bite my lip to keep my mouth from dropping open as she steps away. Instead, I give her a serious nod. "I'll work on that."

She turns, but then spins back around and points

at me. "You made something new, didn't you?"

I nod. "I did."

"It's about damn time. That heron is mine if you ever decide to sell it, so don't you dare unload it while I'm gone." She waves and twirls, disappearing back into her place through the back door. "Be safe! Don't forget to use condoms for group sex!" She shuts and locks it without another backward glance, which is probably good because once more, I'm dumbstruck.

As I climb the curving metal staircase, I shake my head. An octogenarian is living a bigger life than me. Or septuagenarian. Either way, Harriet is grabbing life by the horns and I'm . . . waiting for it to come to me.

It's not until I'm stepping out of the shower that a small voice breaks through my conflicting thoughts. *What if I don't wait? What if I go after it?*

I can't get the possibility out of my head as I wipe the steam from the mirror and face myself.

"Am I done waiting?" I ask my reflection. After a beat, I answer myself. "Yeah, I think I am."

Wrapped in a towel, I pad out to my living area and grab my phone off the table. I find a number I've never had the occasion to use and tap out a text.

TEMPERANCE: *Will I be able to get into the club tonight if I don't have a card?*

My two front teeth worry my lower lip as I set my

phone down on the table. Magnolia Maison doesn't strike me as the type to reply right away.

I force myself to head back into the bathroom and leave it be. That lasts about thirty seconds before I spin around to grab the phone and leave it on the edge of the sink while I do my makeup.

Either way, I'm not going to stay holed up in my apartment tonight. I'm going out, and I'm going to *live*.

CHAPTER 20

Temperance

THE REPLY COMES AS I'M BLOW-DRYING MY HAIR.

MAGNOLIA: *You work up the nerve to come and I'll take care of you.*

It's like she can see inside my head to the warring thoughts.

Don't even consider it.

Bad idea.

Come on, what could it hurt?

Maybe if you just go and watch . . .

She's also right about me having to work up the nerve. It's a full two hours later when the elegant mansion comes into view.

Every time I've come here has been different. The first time, I was completely unprepared. The second time, nervous but excited. This time . . . butterflies the size of turkey vultures flap around in my belly.

I almost chicken out at the gate. But I don't.

I put my Bronco into park and lean on the steering wheel for a few seconds as I contemplate changing my mind for the hundredth time.

Why don't I turn around and drive home? Because once I walk in those doors, I don't have to be me. I don't have to worry about all the responsibilities hanging over my head, the future, or the past.

I never knew I could crave an escape so much. And then there's the man.

Whether he's here or not, he's unleashed something inside me that I never knew existed.

The valet opens the door and I step out, already wearing my mask. I'm finally starting to feel like I belong. Instead of walking up the stairs with wary steps, I climb them with confidence, my stride evidence of my resolve.

I'm ready for whatever comes next.

Magnolia meets me inside the foyer. "Don't you look sassy tonight?" She appraises me from head to toe. "Damn, girl. Where you been hiding that body?"

I opted for a red dress that's been hanging in the back of my closet for a year, unworn and the tags still on. It's red, formfitting, and scandalous.

It suits my mood perfectly.

"Thanks for letting me come tonight."

Something twinkles in her eyes, but I don't know what. Magnolia seems like she has more secrets than the entire Catholic church combined, and I'm not sure I even want to uncover the first layer of them.

"Anything for a friend. You look like you're here to start a fight between all the men who are going to want a piece of you."

I may have thought of one specific man as I dug this dress out of my closet, but that's not something I need to admit.

"I'm just here to watch," I tell her.

"Sure you are, sweet thing. That's what they all say at first." She turns toward the staircase. "But let's get you a tour anyway. See what you came to see."

She leads me up the stairs toward the low, rhythmic music coming from the room I've yet to see.

"Is that . . . the dungeon?" My question comes out more hesitant than I anticipated, and Magnolia glances over her shoulder.

"Dungeon's downstairs. We'll save that for another visit."

I'm not sure whether I'm disappointed or relieved, but anticipation elbows both emotions out of the way as she pushes open the door.

Dark purple lights bathe the room in color, and a DJ is set up on one end. A long, heavy slab of wood stretches the length of one wall, and is manned by two bartenders.

Several conversation areas are set up in small groupings around the room. Most are occupied.

Masked women sit on the laps of men or curl

around other women. There's no full-on nudity, but plenty of skin is showing.

This is where the foreplay happens.

"This is the mingling area. Great place to trawl for a partner if you're in the mood for some variety. You'll always find someone at the bar."

Two men across the room look our way, one nodding at me.

"They're good at scenting fresh meat." She gives me a pointed look. "But as long as you keep it inside the club, you'll be fine. No one would dare step out of line here. You want to stay or do you want to try something else?"

I take another look around the room, feeling self-conscious when I count the number of eyes on me. None of them belong to *him*, though.

I told myself I wasn't going to look for him here. That I didn't care if he was here.

I actually convinced myself of it, but obviously that didn't last long.

"What are my other options?"

Magnolia leads me out of the bar area, and the music quiets when the door closes behind us.

"I think you know what else we have to offer. Private viewing rooms. Rooms where you can be viewed. Rooms where you can be tied up and left to wait for a stranger to come fuck you. Pick your poison."

I'm not sure if she's trying to shock me, but I

refuse to show any surprise. "I want to watch."

"I always knew you had the kink in you. Come with me." She gives me a wicked smile and precedes me up the stairs to the third floor. "If you want to watch but also be comfortable, I have the perfect room for you."

"Okay." My heartbeat accelerates and I tell myself it's because I'm hoofing it up so many stairs again, but even I know that's a bullshit excuse.

The two other doors I've stepped through stand out like beacons, but we don't go toward either of them. Instead, she leads me to a new one.

"I think you'll like what you'll be able to see from here."

She pushes the door open to reveal a large curved leather sectional like you would expect to see in a living room, but instead of facing a television, it's turned toward a viewing window.

"Are all the rooms on this floor for voyeurs?" I ask.

Magnolia nods. "Next level up is all private." She hands me a remote. "Click this, and the window will defrost and you can enjoy. If anyone bothers you, shoot me a text and I'll take care of them."

"Thank you. I appreciate it."

I wait for Magnolia to leave before I make myself comfortable on the center cushion of the sofa.

Before I can talk myself out of it, I press the button on the remote and the window clears, allowing me a perfect view of another room. It looks like something you'd expect to see in a harem, or at least what I'd imagine a harem would have been like. A huge round cushion takes up a large portion of the room, and sheer fabric drapes down from the ceiling.

But it's what's happening on the cushion that sets my blood on fire.

Two men. One woman. She's spread out between them, and four hands roam her naked body while she arches upward.

Holy hell. A ménage.

My thighs clench together as one man, a blond, spreads the woman's legs and kneels between them, dragging his tongue along her skin. She moans as the other man sucks on a nipple, keeping her hair fisted in his hand.

I press back against the cushions, my gaze rapt as the kneeling man peels off her panties.

"So wet. You've been such a good girl. I think it's time I eat this juicy cunt."

I didn't know it was possible for me to go from nervous to soaking wet in under sixty seconds, but, hey, new personal best.

The man looks to the corner of the room as though seeking permission. "You want to see me lick her pussy? Or should we make her wait?"

My attention zeroes in on the shadowed corner of the room, and I squint like it's somehow going to help me see who he's talking to.

There's a chair in the corner. With a man sitting in it.

Instead of responding verbally, a big hand waves them on as though indicating the man should get to work.

Rather than dragging my gaze back to the three-some spread out on the cushion, I focus on the corner. On him.

There's not enough light to see a face, but I can see his hand on his knees, gripping as though fighting for control.

They're big hands, but are they *his*? Is that why Magnolia brought me here?

A tidal wave of contradicting thoughts washes through my brain.

He likes to watch. He made that perfectly clear.

But if he came here tonight . . . why not invite me?

Was the note a lie? Is he done with me?

Ridiculously, a lash of pain swipes across my confidence.

That asshole.

"Aren't you going to come join us?" the man at the woman's breasts says. "You haven't played in a while. I bet you miss the sweet grip of a hungry pussy."

I stand and walk toward the glass, straining to hear his answer. "You better not," I whisper to the empty room, my hands clenching into fists.

Instead of envying the woman with all the attention, I'm consumed with jealousy and want to drag her out by her hair.

What the hell is wrong with me? Why do I care? I can walk my ass right back down to the bar room and pick up a man of my own. He isn't that special.

I spin on my heel and almost wobble right off it when I realize I'm not alone. A man stands just inside the doorway. *My stranger.*

"Why don't you want him to touch her?" The question comes out in almost a mocking tone in that deep, rasping voice. One corner of his mouth curls up in a smirk. "Wishing you had all those hands on you instead?"

"You." It comes out like a curse. "You—"

He pushes off the door and steps toward me, his gaze predatory. "That's right. Me. Only me."

Power rolls off him in waves, and I remember what Magnolia said about him being dangerous.

"I thought you were done with me. Decided to move on to something new and different." I'm not sure what prompts my honesty, but I have nothing to lose by telling the truth.

He doesn't slow, and instinctively, I back up until my shoulders hit the glass of the two-way mirror.

"Why would I move on when I haven't gotten nearly enough of you?" He traps me against the glass, then turns the question around on me. "Why are *you* here? Looking for something new and different?"

I lift my chin. "Maybe I got tired of waiting."

He cups the back of my neck, curling his fingers under my chin. "We can't have that."

He releases his hold on me only to pick me up and lift me into the air.

"What—"

"You wanted to watch, we're going to watch, and I'm going to make you wait until all of them come before you get what you want. Time to teach you some patience."

He settles into the corner cushion of the sofa with me cradled in his arms, both my legs over one thigh and my ass resting on the other.

"But—"

"Watch."

He turns my chin to face the trio, where one man is still trying to get the man in the corner to participate.

"So you thought that was me? Sitting in the corner, getting ready to jack off while I watch them both take her?"

"Maybe," I whisper.

"You were jealous." It's not a question, but a statement.

"Does it matter?" I look up at him and his pale gaze meets mine.

"It makes me fucking hard to know that you were pissed thinking about it."

"Then why the lesson in patience?"

"Because I'm a perverse son of a bitch, and I want to make us both suffer." He drags his tongue over his full bottom lip. "I'm not going to fuck you until you're dying for it. Maybe we'll let them watch us to warm them up for round two."

His suggestion slams into my chest like a freight train. "What? That's not—"

"Not what? Something that makes your pulse hammer?" He reaches out to press his thumb against my throat. "Because you're lying if you say yes."

"I'm not ready for that."

He strokes my skin. "Now *that,* I believe. Watch." He turns my face back toward the window.

One man has his face buried in the woman's pussy, and she moans while the other holds her thighs apart.

"Have you ever imagined what it'd be like to have two men touching you?"

I shake my head.

"Why not?"

I swallow the saliva pooling in my mouth. "Because . . . it seems wrong."

"Is any of it really wrong if everyone's okay with it?"

"I guess not."

The woman's back bows off the cushion, and my inner muscles clench at what she must be feeling.

"I bet you'd scream even louder. Two cocks. Four hands. Might finally tame you. Then again, I'm a greedy motherfucker and I like you wild." He growls the last words, igniting my core, and I shift on his lap. "You like that I want to keep you all to myself. That I'd rather fuck you while they watch, wishing they could have you."

"I don't know." My voice sounds hesitant. Nothing like the bold me who walked in the front door of this place.

"You do, but you haven't admitted it to yourself yet. You will."

The man in the corner stands and approaches the trio.

"My turn." He unbuttons his pants and pulls out his cock. "I want her mouth."

My stranger's hand clasps my ankle before working up my leg to stop on my thigh. "I want your mouth. I want to feel you swallow me down. My cock hitting the back of your throat as you try to take me deeper."

I suck in a breath.

"I jacked off this week imagining fucking your face. You on your knees in front of me. Those dark brown eyes wide as you swallow every last drop."

I tear myself away from the scene to meet his heated gaze. He pushes my dress up my thighs and skims a finger over my pussy.

"Fuck me, you're not wearing panties." His voice deepens, becoming hoarser.

"You stole them last time."

"But you didn't know I'd be here."

"Maybe I was hoping."

His finger traces the seam of my lips as he bites down on his. I reach up and use my fingertip to tug his lip free.

"I want to bite your lip." I don't know where it came from, but my admission is the truth.

"Then what are you waiting for?"

Boldness, the kind that set me on this path tonight, rises up, and I wrap my hand around his neck, pulling him down to me. I drag my teeth over his full lower lip.

His lungs heave, and before I can finish what I started, he pushes a thick finger inside me. I turn my head into his shoulder as he fucks in and out of me.

"Not. Fair." I bite out the words, my teeth digging into the muscle hidden beneath the soft fabric.

"Don't ever expect me to play fair."

He brings me all the way to the edge, clenching around him, before he pulls away.

"Wait—"

"No, I want you to come on my face." He moves me off his lap and goes to his knees on the floor. "Watch them and imagine they're watching you."

That's all he says before he buries his face between my legs, lashing me with his tongue.

I attempt to focus on the scene in front of me. The woman is on her knees, her hands on the thighs of the man from the corner, as one of the other men takes her from behind. The third man sits on the cushion, his hand wrapped around his cock, watching. But instead of watching them, he's staring directly at the window as though he can see right through it to me.

A shiver races down my spine, but instead of being scared, I revel in it.

What if he could see me? What would I do?

I spread my legs wider, and my stranger groans in approval.

He pulls back. "You taste so fucking good." He uses his thumbs to part my lips, and then one of his thumbs ventures into no man's land, skimming over my virgin hole.

"What—"

His eyes flare with heat as I jump. He says nothing as he does it again, spreading my own slickness across it.

I squirm on the couch, trying to pull away.

"Goddamn, you're sweet." His lips curl into a smirk. "But taking your ass for the first time is going to be even sweeter."

"How do you know I haven't—" I attempt to sound more experienced, but my words are cut off as he adds pressure to his thumb, almost breaching the tight ring.

"Because you can't hold still. Not sure if you want to run, or push back and find out exactly how it feels. Don't worry, I'll take good care of you."

He lowers his face back between my legs, sucking my clit and teasing my asshole until I'm ready to break apart. I can't focus on the scene before me. I don't care about anything but the orgasm that's bearing down on me.

As I arch my back and embrace it, he pushes the tip of his thumb into my ass, warping the pleasure into something even hotter.

My moan turns sharp on the edges, a cross between a scream and a plea for mercy.

But he has none. He keeps pushing me until my body goes limp.

When he rises to his feet, he wipes his mouth with the back of his hand. "Now you're ready."

He picks me up and carries me around the back of the sofa and presses me forward. He yanks my dress up over my ass, and I hear the crinkle of foil as the room on the other side of the window goes black.

"What's going on?" I ask. His comment from earlier, *what if they could see us*, comes to the forefront of my thoughts.

"Put on a show. Let them know just how damn good it feels. Let them hear it."

"But—"

"I dare you." He reaches around the front of my dress and tugs down the neckline, letting my tits spill free. "I won't share you, but I'll let you pretend."

When he pushes inside me, I imagine the four of them watching me. It's a fantasy I didn't know I had.

When I come again, it's even harder than before, and I know it's because of *him*.

Not the club. Not the games.

Just. Him.

Shit.

CHAPTER 21

Temperance

H E LOWERS ME ONTO THE COUCH AND STRIDES toward a connected room. When I hear water running, I assume that it's a bathroom.

The first time I was here, when he stepped out of the room, I ran like I'd been scalded. Tonight, though, I hate the idea of leaving. I hate the idea of him leaving. I want to stay and soak this up and pretend it's more than what it is.

I can't get attached. I just can't. I repeat what I know is the absolute truth as he returns with a washcloth and offers it to me.

But I am. I think about him all the time, and . . .

"I don't even know your name," I blurt out.

He pauses, his fingers on the buttons of his shirt, and looks at me. "So? Does that really matter?"

His response hits me like a wrecking ball, and I want to scream, *Yes, it matters.*

What we're doing here isn't normal. It isn't a relationship. There's no connection between us beyond what happens in this club. I thought I could handle that. Really, I thought I could, which is why I searched for a place like this. But now . . . it feels different. My expectations and reality don't align.

I didn't want a relationship. I don't have time. But I've also never been the kind of girl who can have more than a one-night stand and have it mean nothing, not that I have much experience with those situations anyway. It's either one night of fun and done, or *more*. This isn't even friends with benefits, *because we're not friends.* To be friends, I'd have to know his name. Hell, to even be a fuck-buddy, I'd have to know his name.

I can't do this.

As much as I want to tell myself I can, I know it's a lie.

"Yeah, it really does."

He studies me as though waiting for me to say something else. "It hasn't mattered yet."

I bite down on my lip. "I know. I thought . . . I thought I could do the casual thing. Take my fun and not get attached."

His expression intensifies. "And?"

"I can't do this and not need some kind of genuine connection."

"What we just had." He gestures between us. "That was a pretty fucking genuine connection. You can't tell me you don't feel it."

I look away, up at the ceiling. "Of course I feel it. But I can't keep doing this without feeling more. You're a guy I met randomly in a *sex club*, for God's sake. Whatever we're doing here can never go outside the club. But I can't keep coming back and then not think about you for the rest of the week. This doesn't work for me. I'm done."

His blue gaze sharpens on me. "You think you can walk away now and not want more?"

"That's the problem! I already want more, and it's not going to happen." I school my features and inject confidence into my tone. "So, I'm done. I'm not coming back. It's over."

He walks toward me and my muscles tense. *Fight or flight.* When he crouches low, I curl my fingers into the skirt of my dress to keep from fidgeting.

"Bullshit."

I glare at him. "No bullshit."

"You think this is just going to die? That cutting it off like that is going to make you stop thinking about me? It won't. I've got a hell of a lot more experience with this shit than you do, and what's happening here isn't your normal weekend club fuck."

"I don't need to hear about—"

"Maybe you do. Because I shouldn't be thinking about you after I walk out this door either. I *never* think about anyone after I walk out this fucking door. But you . . ." He pauses, and I don't know what to say.

"So, what does that mean? That you're going to show up at my front door and take me on a date, and this can be more?"

He rears back like I just told him to go fuck himself. His look of shock is so ridiculous that I can't help but burst out in absurd laughter. He rises and turns toward the viewing window, giving me his back. I can't read his posture because I don't know him at all.

"See? This is why I have to stop. I'm not going to be the girl who has a fling and gets attached to a guy who can't commit, and then gets her heart broken. I'm a realist. Even if I believed in happily-ever-afters, this story wouldn't come with one."

He raises his arms and grips the back of his neck, the muscles of his shoulders and back straining. "You don't understand." The words sound like they're grated out from between clenched teeth. When he spins around, the vein in his forehead pulses. "My life is complicated."

I shrug like it's no big thing, but the generic excuse unleashes a wave of disappointment that eats at me like battery acid. Not that I'm surprised. No one's going to break their habits or routine for me. I'm not that kind of girl.

"Well, guess what? My life is complicated too. So I'm going to uncomplicate it a little and say good-bye."

I wipe my sweaty hands on my dress and rise. I turn and round the couch to slip on my heels and grab my purse. When I reach the door, I glance over my shoulder, and his back is to me once again.

"Good luck with your complicated life."

I twist the handle and pull it open two inches before it slams shut and his arms bracket my body, trapping me against the door.

"You really think you're going to forget this? Me? How it feels to come so hard, you can't remember your own name?"

I force indifference into my voice. "I'll live without it."

"Maybe. But you'll still crave it. I give you a week before you're back here, looking for me again like you were tonight."

My anger flares and I turn in his arms, meeting his intense stare. "You know what I'm really good at? Proving people wrong."

CHAPTER 22

Temperance

I HATE MYSELF FOR WALKING AWAY.

He's right. I can't stop thinking about him. He haunts my dreams for the rest of the weekend, no matter how many Chris Hemsworth movies I watch. When I get to the distillery on Monday, I'm determined to throw myself into work and forget all of it.

By Thursday, I'm finally able to go thirty minutes without thinking about him or the club. I wave off Keira as she climbs into the back of a chauffeur-driven car, heading off on vacation, with her orders to call me if I need anything, and I breathe a sigh of relief.

I can do this. I'm a capable COO. Life is great.

Then a messenger arrives an hour later, and my determination implodes.

The handwriting on the outside of the envelope is familiar, and I tell myself to throw it in the trash without opening it. But I'm weak and completely un-supervised. I use my letter opener to slice the top and dump out the contents.

A single card, just like the one he gave me the night of the fundraiser. A date and time are written on it.

Tomorrow.

Just the thought of it heats my blood, and my thighs clench together.

No. I'm not going. As a matter of fact, I'm going to make other plans so I'm not remotely tempted.

I pull out my phone and scroll through my con-tacts. The list is remarkably short. That's what hap-pens when you walk away from your old life and cut off communication with pretty much everyone from your past, and you're not that great at making friends to begin with.

My brother.

My boss.

My landlady.

A few distillery employees.

A notorious madam.

Valentina Hendrix.

The gallery owner's contact information taunts me, but for a completely different reason. I've been driving around with the phoenix in the back of my Bronco since Elijah helped me load it up, and I told myself it's because I can't unload it myself. That's only partially the truth.

The rest of the story is that I'm still working up the courage to take it to Noble Art and show it to Valentina on behalf of *my friend*, the artist.

Before I can talk myself out of it, I tap CALL. She answers on the third ring, right before I lose my nerve and hang up.

"Hello?"

"Hi, this is Temperance Ransom."

"Temperance! I'd almost given up hope on you calling, and I've had no luck finding any information on the artist who created that piece. I was going to give you until tomorrow before I came back to harass you."

"I have another piece," I say. "I mean, I have one you can see, if you want."

"Really?" Her excitement practically vibrates over the connection.

"Yes."

"When?"

I glance at the clock. "I can be there in about a half hour."

"Perfect!" There's a muted clapping noise in the background. "I'll be here. You just made my day."

We hang up, and I immediately wonder if I've made a huge mistake. Maybe I should have offered to text a picture to her just in case she thought it was hideous, and I wouldn't have to see her face when she sees it in person.

Coward, my inner voice says, mocking me.

Woman up. You know you did a damn good job. Besides, if you can't own this dream, do you really deserve it?

I draw in a deep, steadying breath. "I can do this," I tell the empty office. "And I better do it now before I lose my nerve." With a final glance at the card on my desk, I sweep it into the trash and go to the filing cabinet to retrieve my purse.

"Time to put up or shut up." I lock my door behind me, let the receptionist on duty know I'm leaving, and head for the parking lot.

"Where is it?" Valentina asks the moment I walk through the door of Noble Art.

It took me twenty-five minutes to fight traffic from a funeral to get into the Quarter and find a parking spot, and another five to hoof it two blocks.

"Do you want to see a picture first?" I've thought about this for the last half hour. The best way to see the phoenix for the first time isn't to view it lying down in the back of my Bronco.

"You have one?" Her eyes light up. "Why didn't you send it to me? Let's see it."

I retrieve my phone from my purse and pull up the picture I took in the workshop at Elijah's, but keep the screen turned toward me. "It's not a professional photo, or anything."

"Temperance, show me the damn picture."

I hand over the phone, and she's silent for three of the longest seconds of my life.

"Wow."

"Is that a good wow or bad wow?" I don't mean to ask the question aloud, but it's out before I can stop it.

Valentina doesn't look up from my phone. Instead, she zooms in closer on the photo. "It's a good wow. This is so unique."

"They're all one of a kind. Pretty much impossible to replicate."

She finally drags her attention from the screen to me. "Level with me here. What's it going to take for me to buy this?"

"I don't know . . ." I trail off and my gaze bounces around the gallery, cataloging all the beautiful artwork that seems *real* in comparison to what's always been a hobby for me. "Do you really think one of your clients would buy it?"

Her stare pins me. "We were at the same auction, right?"

"Right, but it was put up under someone else's name."

"Whose name should it have been under?"

It's the moment of truth. *Do I tell her or do I lie?*

I take a deep breath. "Mine."

Valentina's lips stretch into a wide smile and she pumps a fist in the air. "I was right!" Her reaction is nothing like I expected.

"You knew?"

"I guessed. I know a little bit about hiding your creations because you're not ready to take ownership of them out in the public eye." She points to a wall with several nude paintings. "Those are mine."

I can feel my eyebrows climb to my hairline. "Really?"

She nods. "Yes, and I didn't think they were good enough to display here, but someone else took that choice out of my hands, and even though I wanted to strangle him at the time, he was right. How long have you been making stuff like this?"

Her question drags me out of present day, out of the gallery, and deposits me back in the past about fifteen years earlier.

⊷————·————⊶

"What the fuck did you do with my soldering iron?"

I jumped as the door to the workshop slammed against the outside, shaking the entire building on its rickety foundation. I dropped the solder and the iron, then scooped up my little creation and tucked it behind my back, my eyes stinging with tears as the burning metal touched my arm.

"Nothing."

"Lying little bitch. I need it. Now." Dad's words were already slurring, telling me he'd hit the sauce today already.

"It's right here. Sorry. I'll get out of here."

His sneer, one of his three facial expressions—the cruel smirk or the thundercloud of anger completed the trio—revealed a wad of dip in his lip. "You been in my shit again? Is that why I'm missing parts, because you're stealing from me? Is that what I taught you?"

I shook my head until I thought my eyeballs would bounce out of their sockets.

His hand swung out and the back of it caught my cheek, snapping my head sideways. "Told you not to lie to me, girl."

I stumbled back and lost my grip on my creation. It fell to the plank floor with a clatter.

"The fuck is that?" Moving faster than I'd seen him move in ages, Dad swiped it up.

"I was just—"

He studied the two little people I'd made. A guy and a girl. They were holding hands.

He glanced up at me. "You took two fucking spark plugs and some fuses to make this piece of shit? First, the scrap metal that'd be better off in my pocket as some change, and now you're using shit I actually need for your waste of time?" He sets it on the workbench and reaches for a hammer on its hook.

"Dad, no. I'll buy new ones. That's—"

I couldn't even get out my explanation that it was a gift for Mama for her birthday before he swung and shattered it, spark plugs and all.

"Look what you made me do, girl! Look." He shoved the broken metal and ceramic in my face, not caring that a sharp edge nicked me and I jumped back. I reached up to touch the smarting spot, and my fingers came away red.

"That should teach you to fuck with shit that ain't yours again. If it scars, then you'll never forget."

He snatched up the soldering iron and tossed my people to the floor.

"Quit wasting your time on those pieces of shit. You got better things to do. Like get a job. No one's ever gonna pay you for that junk except the scrap yard."

Dad turned and left the shack of a workshop, leaving both my junk and me crushed.

⊷———— • ————⊷

The memory is depressing as hell, but something that feels a lot like vindication bubbles up in my gut. He said no one would ever pay for my stuff but the scrap yard, and he's dead wrong.

That brings a smile to my face, and I wish he was still around so I could prove him wrong.

"Temperance?" Valentina says.

"Sorry, just counting back. It's been a lot of years. Really, since I was a kid. It was something to do. A way to keep myself entertained."

"Well, I'd say that it has the potential to be much more. Now, let's go look at it."

Shaking off the memory, I give her a bright smile. "More sounds pretty great to me. It's in the back of my Bronco. I parked a few blocks away."

The excitement on her face mirrors mine. "I've got a reserved spot in the alley. Why don't you go get your car and pull up there? It'll be easier to bring it inside too."

"Okay." My reply sounds coherent, but inside, I'm doing cartwheels and blocking out the image of my dad breaking everything he ever saw that I made. *Screw you, Dad.*

When I walk out the door, I can't even believe that I'm going to get my Bronco to sell my artwork to a *real gallery.*

See, old man, you were wrong.

Laughter bubbles up in my chest, and I practically skip to where I parked.

My stomach drops to the pavement and curls into a tight knot as I search for my Bronco. But it's gone, and all that's left is an empty parking spot.

CHAPTER 23

Temperance

THIS CAN'T BE HAPPENING.

I blink, looking around as though I forgot where I parked. But I didn't. I know exactly where I parked, and it's gone. *Gone.*

People walk up and down the street but no one makes eye contact. There's a kid on the corner playing for tips on a couple of five-gallon buckets. He must have just set up shop, because he wasn't there when I parked.

"Hey! You!" I call out, interrupting his drum solo.

He looks up at me. "What?"

"Did you see an old Bronco across the street?"

He twirls his drumstick and shrugs.

I suck in a breath and reach into my purse to pull out a five and shove it at him. "Did you see it?"

"Maybe."

With an animalistic growl building in my throat,

I grab a twenty and hold it just out of reach. "Come on, kid. This matters."

He bounces up quicker than I expected and snatches it from my hand. "It was there. Now it's gone."

"Who took it?"

Another shrug. "Don't know. Didn't pay much mind to it."

"You saw nothing? At all?"

He tilts his head to the side. "It's a fuck-ton safer for me to see nothing, lady. I gotta live out here. You don't."

My entire body practically vibrates with helpless rage. "Fine." I pull out my business card and drop it in his hat where he's collecting tips. "If you remember anything, call any number on there."

He rolls his eyes. "Yeah. I'll get right on that."

I turn and walk away, my eyes smarting with the need to let tears fall. My best shot at my dream just disappeared with whoever drove away with my fucking car.

I pull out my phone and hit Rafe's number. It goes immediately to voice mail, doesn't even ring. *What the hell?* I hang up and call again. Same thing happens. This time, I leave a message.

"Rafe. I need you. Please. Call me."

I hang up and immediately dial a number I deleted long ago, but still know by heart.

He answers on the first ring and skips the polite

greeting. "You change your mind?"

"I need your help."

I trudge back to the gallery with nothing but Elijah's promise to make some calls to see if he can find my car. Valentina pops her head out of the back room when the front door chimes signal my entrance, and her face creases with confusion.

"Couldn't find the spot?"

"Not exactly." I'm not proud, but that's the moment a few of my tears finally sneak free. "Someone stole my car."

"Oh shit! Honey, I'm so sorry." This woman, who I barely know, crosses the room and throws her arms around me. "It's okay. It'll be okay. I'll call my husband. He'll get the cops on it, and they'll find it."

I jerk my head up at the word *cops*. Where I'm from, we don't call the cops. And working at the distillery, that's certainly not my first inclination either.

"Cops?"

Valentina steps back and tilts her head to the side. "Yeah, unless you've got a bunch of illegal weapons or drugs in it. If that's the case, definitely don't tell me."

Shockingly, her statement rattles a laugh out of me.

"No. Nothing illegal. Just . . . my sculpture.

Which no car thief is going to want. They'll probably toss it out as garbage."

"And then we'll kill them. I mean, catch them. Hold on."

She walks to a desk at the back of the gallery and picks up her phone. She taps out something on the screen.

When it rings moments later, she answers, "That was quick. Can you come to the gallery? No, everything's fine, but I need a cop and I don't want to call the precinct." She pauses. "I'll explain when you get here."

When she hangs up, she looks at me. "My husband will be here shortly. Just has to pack up the baby gear first. In the meantime, is there anyone else you want to call?"

I think of my brother, who is undoubtedly doing something illegal, and then my boss . . . who is most certainly on a plane right now. "Not really."

"Then I think you need a drink."

"I should probably say no . . ."

"Pshh. Stop that. You need it. You're practically shaking. Now, sit." Valentina nods to the chair in front of her desk before she disappears into the back room. A few moments later, she returns with a wine bottle and a champagne flute. "I know this is more of a hard-liquor situation, but prosecco is all I have at the moment."

"Thank you."

She pours the wine with a steady hand, and I try to stop mine from shaking.

"I just can't believe . . ." I trail off and take a sip.

"Honey, this is New Orleans. I'm sure a car gets stolen down here every day. Rix doesn't work that beat, but I'm sure he could back me up with figures."

As I drink in silence for a few minutes, she tells me a few stories about artists whose pieces are for sale in the gallery, including her part-time employee who's in art school.

I'm halfway through my second glass of prosecco when a beautiful man who could practically double for Shemar Moore walks in the door with a baby strapped to his chest. His silver gaze cuts to Valentina, and he wastes no time closing the distance between them.

"What's going on? Who do I need to kill for interrupting the little man's dinner?"

Valentina rises. "There are my two favorite guys. Thanks for coming down so quick."

He pulls her in close to his body and leans down to press a kiss to her lips. "Always, duchess. What the hell is going on?"

I stare at them with a longing I didn't know I could feel. This beautiful badass of a man is charging to her rescue, complete with a smiling baby. My ovaries are toast.

"This is Temperance. She works at—"

"Seven Sinners, for Mount's woman," he finishes

for her, his eyes narrowing on me.

I nod, not feeling the same welcome in his tone that came from Valentina. "That's right."

"You here to cause trouble? Because we don't need it," he says, and a shaft of disappointment shoots through me.

"Rix!" Valentina smacks him on the shoulder. "Be nice. She's had a crap day. She came to show me a sculpture, and someone stole her car."

He studies me with suspicion rolling off him in waves.

"It's okay. I'll get help from someone who doesn't look at me like I'm a criminal." I lower the glass to the desk and grab my purse. "Sorry to waste your time, Valentina."

I've taken two steps when he speaks.

"Why didn't you call your boss? Pretty sure you'd find your car a hell of a lot faster that way."

I look over my shoulder. "They just left to go on vacation. This isn't an emergency worth bothering them over. I can handle it myself."

His brows dive together. "Really? Pretty sure Mount would have heads rolling for this."

"Not necessary, but don't worry. I'll figure it out. I'll head to the precinct to file a report and call my insurance company."

"Oh no. You're not leaving. He's helping you, and he's going to be nice about it too." Valentina's voice brooks no disagreement.

"Is that right?" He reaches out and clasps his wife's hand with the baby between them. "She one of your people now? Adopting her?"

I'm not sure what he means, but when Valentina nods, his face relaxes and he smiles at her.

"Shoulda figured. Only for you, duchess. Only for you." He presses a kiss to the back of her hand and releases it before turning back to me. "Give me all the vehicle details and I'll get a BOLO out. If it's rolling around, we'll get a call. I'll let my boys know it's priority."

"Make sure you tell them that there's a very valuable piece of artwork in the back, and I will personally bake cookies for whoever makes sure that sculpture comes back unharmed," Valentina tells him as she presses a kiss to the baby's head.

Rix smiles again, this time laughing. "Duchess, I thought you wanted them to bring the art back, not make sure you never see it again."

Valentina growls at him and reaches for the baby, and my heart pangs with envy.

I want that.

CHAPTER 24

Temperance

TWENTY-FOUR HOURS AND NO SIGN OF MY Bronco, and Elijah says it hasn't shown up in any chop shop in town that he knows. He's still looking, and so are the cops. I've left three more messages on my brother's phone—which never rings before kicking me to voice mail—and sent him a dozen texts. I've gotten zero replies.

It's not unusual for him to go radio silent for a few days every once in a while, but he always tells me first and then gets back to me as soon as he can. My gut says this is different. *Bad different.* Or maybe that's just my stomach churning from the fact someone stole my damn Bronco.

Keira kept her promise to Mount and never called work today, and I decided to wait until Monday to tell her about my car.

Surely, I'll find it before then, right? I sure as hell

hope so.

When I climb into a taxi on Friday night, part of me wants to go straight to the club and wait until my appointed time and let my stranger help me forget this shitty end of my week.

But I'm not doing it.

I can't keep meeting a guy whose name I don't know. That's definitely not going to end with me having a man who looks at me like Rix does at Valentina.

If I can't call him for help, then he doesn't deserve to be part of my life. Simple enough.

And since I don't have any way to contact him, in addition to not having his name, my decision is made.

It's over.

As I ride back to my place, I can't help but wonder if he'll find someone else to play with when I don't show up.

Stop thinking about him.

My phone rings as I toss my purse on the counter. Valentina's name is on the screen, and hope rushes through me.

"Valentina? Did they find my car?"

"Oh, honey, sorry, no. They didn't."

That hope instantly deflates. "Oh."

"But I was wondering . . . do you have plans tonight?"

I look around all five hundred square feet of my apartment—from the living area to the kitchenette and to the doorway to the bedroom—as though searching for an excuse, which is my knee-jerk reaction. Then I remind myself that I *need* plans tonight, because that may be the only way I keep my promise to myself not to go to Haven.

"No."

"Good. Well, maybe not good for you, but good for us because I'm having some friends over for a girls' night tonight. I was telling a few of them about you, and we thought you might want to join us."

Girls' night? That's one of those things that I've seen in movies and read about in books but haven't actually ever done. Not even in college, because I was working three jobs just to pay tuition and rent.

"Uh, sure?" My answer comes out as a question, and I clear my throat. "I mean, I'd love to."

"Great. I'll text you my address." She pauses, and I can practically feel her wince at reminding me of the fact that I don't have a way to get there. "Wait, never mind that. I can have someone pick you up."

"I can get there. It's no big deal. What time?"

She fills me in on the rest of the details, and when I hang up, I force myself to smile.

Now I won't be tempted to go to the club.

⊶———— · ————⊷

I have no idea what I've gotten myself into. None at all.

First, Valentina's place is a beautiful house in the Garden District that I guarantee costs more than I'll probably ever make in my entire life. Property here isn't cheap, especially when it's perfectly restored like hers.

Keira would probably feel comfortable here, but I feel insanely out of place. I wipe my heels three times on the doormat out of old habit to avoid tracking mud inside onto the hardwood floors and expensive-looking rugs. Canvases of gorgeous nudes, which I recognize as Valentina's own work from the gallery, decorate the walls.

They're incredible. It's even more incredible to think that she makes her living from art and it can pay for this life of hers. Or at least I assume, considering her husband is a cop. Then again, I probably shouldn't assume anything about anything.

"Welcome," Valentina says, giving me a quick hug. "I'm so glad you could make it." She follows my gaze to the paintings on the walls. "Yes, those are mine too. Rix insists that I showcase them here. He's actually the one who made me finally take the leap to sell them. He changed everything for me. I would've kept them hidden in my studio for the rest of my life if it'd been left up to me to find the courage. You get me, I know."

I swallow, thinking about what a crazy leap of faith that must have been, because I'm still having trouble comprehending it. "Clearly, you made the right choice."

She smiles. "You are too. I promise. I have instincts for art, and I know yours is going to sell. It's unique and raw and beautiful. People are going to die for it. You just wait."

I'm still soaking up her compliments when she points toward the living room. "Come on. I can't wait to introduce you to everyone."

Valentina leads me into a beautiful room and introduces me to a trio of women so quickly, I don't catch a single one of their names. They're all ridiculously gorgeous and look like they could rule the world as a hobby.

I sit down and stay quiet, listening to them chatter about their husbands and boyfriends and what sounds like amazing lives.

One of them is literally married to a billionaire. *A freaking billionaire.* She's also wearing the cutest purple vintage cocktail dress I've ever seen.

"Temperance works at Seven Sinners," Valentina informs them as part of my introduction.

"They have incredible whiskey cocktails," the gorgeous redhead says, wearing leggings and an off-the-shoulder sweatshirt that says REVENGE OF THE NERDS on it. "Rhett took me on a date there."

I'm trying to remember her name and failing, but I latch onto the one thing I can actually talk about and not sound like an idiot—whiskey. "We do. Even if you're not a whiskey drinker, they're pretty delicious cocktails."

The redhead must realize I can't remember her name. "I'm Ariel, by the way. And before you ask, yes, I'm named after *The Little Mermaid*. I've got thingamabobs aplenty, and I always want more." She winks.

"She means laptops aplenty so she can hack into government databases," Valentina says.

"Shhh. Don't tell her all my secrets yet. I save those for the second date," Ariel replies with a laugh.

One of the women, an intimidating blonde named Vanessa, waves her off good-naturedly. "We're talking whiskey first, not hacking. I need to buy a case of that Phoenix label. Con loves it, and I want to surprise him. If you could hook me up, I would be a very grateful woman."

Her question actually makes me feel useful here, which is nice. "I'm happy to."

"Fabulous. I'm holding you to it. What's your number?"

When I tell her, she puts it in her phone and fires off a text to me so I have hers. *I'm making friends.* It's a little astonishing, but totally cool.

"Now, how about we stop badgering her for booze and drink some of our own. After all, y'all have designated drivers tonight, right?"

The wine and other drinks are refilled, and I'm three glasses into some very delicious red wine before I realize it.

"I overheard the craziest conversation at the shop today. You won't even believe it," the woman married to the billionaire says. I believe her name is Yve.

Valentina fills me in. "Yve owns Dirty Dog, and she just opened a brand-new lingerie store attached to it. You have to check it out."

"And the gossip in Pretty Kitty is the *best*," Yve says.

"So, spill," Valentina says. The chatter in the room hushes.

"I heard about a sex club. Outside of town. Super fancy and expensive. The kind that I can't believe Lucas wouldn't already know about. No one's supposed to talk about it, but this woman accidentally let it slip while she was trying on corsets."

"I bet she gets her membership yanked. They're not supposed to talk about it," I say before catching myself. Every eye in the room focuses on me. "I mean, I assume that's how those places work."

Yve's eyebrows go up. "You've been there. Haven't you?"

As I open my mouth to deny it, Valentina refills my glass. "She's a terrible liar, for the record."

"Hey! That's not fair."

Valentina rolls her eyes. "Seriously? Trying to pretend that wasn't your artwork the night of the auction? Pshh. You need to work on those skills if you want to lie worth a damn."

I take a rather unladylike swig of wine. "I am not

a bad liar. I'm a great liar."

Yve smirks. "Then prove it. Two truths and a lie. You're up."

I freeze, wondering what the hell I've gotten myself into. To buy time, I drain the glass, which probably isn't the smartest move.

"I've never seen an uncircumcised penis. My middle name is Aurelia. It's been six years since I committed a felony." They spill out of me quicker than I was able to down the wine.

Mouths around the room drop open.

"She's a terrible liar."

"And a felon."

Valentina bursts out laughing. "Only if she got caught. I have a feeling Temperance is too smart for that."

"I don't know what you're talking about."

Yve, the shop owner, pipes up. "Sure thing, Temperance who hasn't seen enough penises in her life. Now, tell us about the club. If I can rustle up more business catering to these ladies, I need to know."

I bite down on my lip, but the wine has loosened my tongue. "I can't. It's against the rules. You don't talk about it."

The blonde, Vanessa, reaches for the wine. "Wait, so it's like fight club?"

"No, it's . . . probably way more dangerous than fight club."

"So, who'd you bang? How many?" This question

comes from Yve.

"Just one guy. I don't know his name."

"You *whore*. I think I love you," Vanessa says and turns to Valentina. "She's in the girl gang, by the way. We needed an actual rule-breaker instead of a pretend rule-breaker like you. Who knows when we might need to commit a felony and not get caught. But I vote that Temperance doesn't talk to the cops. You get to do that."

The women all nod, and a wave of acceptance engulfs me, but I know I shouldn't get used to it.

"He was at the auction," I tell Valentina. "That was the only time I ever saw him outside the club."

Her eyes sparkle with interest. "What did he look like?"

"Besides gorgeous in a suit? Dark hair, blue eyes, broad shoulders."

"The asshole who outbid me on your piece? Are you joking?"

My mouth drops open this time. "What? He did not."

She nods. "Dark gray pinstripe three-piece suit. Light blue shirt that made his eyes pop. Uh, yeah. That was him. I contemplated sketching him for Rix so I could track him down to buy it from him."

The knowledge sends me reeling. *My stranger bought my artwork?*

"That's . . . no way."

"Yes. I swear."

"Then I have his company name somewhere. I wonder . . ."

Ariel pipes up. "If you have the company name, I can track him down in less than five minutes."

"Ari, I'm pretty sure Rhett told you no more hacking." This comes from Valentina.

"This is barely hacking. It's for the sisterhood. Shouldn't she at least know the name of the guy she fucked? I mean . . . what if she got pregnant or something. It's practically required."

"I'm definitely not pregnant." I look down at my wineglass. "I don't think. I hope. No, definitely not."

"That's probably for the best," Ariel says. I can practically see her fingers twitching, like she wants a keyboard in front of her. "So, what's the company name?"

My mind goes blank as I try to remember it, but all I can picture is his glacier-blue eyes. "I don't remember."

"Get it for me tomorrow and I'll go digging." She glances at Valentina. "This one doesn't like it when I bring my computer, so I left it at home."

"Do you have any idea how much trouble we could get in if you brought it with? I am married to a cop."

That's when I decide girls' night is basically the best invention ever. Right behind multiple orgasms. And men with no names who won't be able to hide for long.

CHAPTER 25

Temperance

"THANKS FOR THE RIDE."

"You sure you don't want me to walk you up?" Rix sounds a little concerned when he watches from the driver's side of his Suburban as I lean on the gate.

"I'm fine. I promise."

"I'll wait until I see the light come on inside."

The man is quite the gentleman, and I'm still marveling at the insane coincidence that Valentina has not one, but *two* friends who have lived in the apartment that I rent from Harriet. Neither of them were able to make it to girls' night, but she promised me they'd be at the next one.

The next one.

I made friends. And it felt really good.

Buzzing from the wine and the feeling of acceptance, I unlock the gate and close it behind me before waving at Rix and heading down the path to the courtyard. As I climb the stairs, I hang on to the railing for dear life so I don't fall to my death.

I'm not ready to die. I've got another girls' night to go to and a man to track down.

A voice comes out of the shadows when I hit the top, practically sending me into cardiac arrest.

"You hanging with cops now, Tempe?"

"Oh my God!" I screech before I realize it's Elijah.

"Jesus Christ, woman."

"You scared the hell out of me!"

"And here I thought you'd be happy to find out that I got a line on your Bronco."

Excitement flares inside me. "Really?"

"Temperance? You okay? Thought I heard you yell." It's Rix's voice coming through the bars of my gate by the sidewalk.

"That the cop?" Elijah says, keeping his voice low.

"I'm fine," I call out to Rix. "Saw a rat the size of a cat. I'm heading in now. Thanks!"

I shove my hand into my purse and find my keys. Elijah takes them from my hand when I fail to get the key into the lock on my second try.

"You're sauced."

"It's none of your damn business what I am," I tell him when I flip on the light.

"It is if you're going to puke in my car when we go for a ride."

I turn and look at him. "Where?"

"You want your Bronco back or not?"

"That's a stupid question."

"Then we wait for the cop to leave, and we're out of here."

I narrow my gaze on him, but there are still two Elijahs in my apartment. "Are you lying to me? Is this some kind of trick?"

"You called me for help. Remember?"

My fuzzy brain attempts to remember what I did five minutes ago, and beyond that is nearly impossible.

"Hold on." I stumble to the living area and plop ungracefully onto the small settee.

"You're gonna puke."

"Shut up. I'm not seventeen anymore and running from the cops. I didn't do anything wrong."

Elijah leans against the countertop, staring at me. "You did help me chop a car last week . . ."

"Shut up."

"You always were—"

Whatever Elijah is saying fades away as my lids droop and my body grows heavy.

"Dammit, Tempe."

CHAPTER 26

Temperance

MY EYELIDS FLUTTER LIKE BUTTERFLIES weighted down with lead balloons, and I raise my arms to stretch. In the process, my hand smacks into something warm.

"Damn, girl."

My eyes pop open as I turn my head, staring in shock at the form next to me in bed. Elijah covers his nose, which apparently I just punched.

"Oh my God. What the hell?" I scramble up to a seated position, and as the sheet falls to reveal *everything*, I screech again. "What did you do, Elijah Joseph Devereux? If you touched me, I'm going to kill you!"

His sleep-rumpled hair flops over his forehead, and his lips curl into a lopsided grin as I grab the sheet and yank it up over my chest.

"Well, last night—" he says.

My hand shoots out to hover over the nightstand. "I'll have my finger on a trigger in less than three seconds, so you might want to think real carefully about what you're going to say."

His grin, shockingly, widens. "You're always so damn sexy when you're threatening to shoot me. Goddamn, you're beautiful, Tempe. It's like a punch to the gut seeing you like this again." His gaze starts at my messy bedhead and drags down my face to where my hand clutches the sheet to my nakedness. "I miss you. A hell of a lot."

Even though the words wrap around me like a warm blanket, I'm not the girl Elijah misses. I haven't been her in a long time.

When I don't reply, he leans closer, the sheet pooling around his lap. *Jesus Christ, tell me he isn't naked.*

"I didn't touch you, but damn, did I want to." His bare chest rises and falls, and he sounds sincerer than I think he ever has. "I want to so fucking bad."

He ducks his head like he's coming in for a kiss, and the split-second decision faces me. *Go back or go forward.*

I may not have a clue what's in my future, because apparently my mystery man isn't going to be part of it, but I know Elijah's in my past.

"Put some clothes on, Eli." I yank the sheet, wrapping it around myself, and scramble out of the bed.

He reclines, completely uncaring that I just

yanked the sheet off him and he's sporting morning wood in the morning light. "You sure you want to do that?"

Elijah is nothing if not cocky.

I turn away. "Clothes, Eli. And feel lucky I didn't shoot you for stripping me naked while I was unconscious."

He sighs. "So, it's like that? Not even a thank-you?"

I head for the bathroom and shoot him a glare over my bare shoulder. "It's been like that since you decided to show Lindsey Jo the backseat of your truck when I was seventeen and dumb enough to think about giving up all my plans for you."

Elijah pops up, his shoulders squared, and I keep my attention on his face.

"And you think that was an accident, Temperance? You think I didn't know exactly what I was doing?"

"What do you mean?" My fingers grip the sheet tightly enough to tear holes through it.

His eyes narrow. "If I left the choice on the table, me or college, we both know you would've tried to do both. And then when shit got too hard, you would've dropped out. You think I wanted to be responsible for that? For you letting go of your dream, and watching the resentment build every time you had to pull a double shift at Rickety to help make ends meet? I didn't want that for you."

My mouth drops open. "You did it . . . on purpose?"

Elijah's sharp nod tears off a web of lies covering my past to reveal the truth. "Sure as fuck did. Could barely get my dick hard knowing that as soon as I touched her, I was giving up the best thing that could ever happen to me. Because I wanted better for you." His gaze drops to the bed. "Still want better for you."

The swirl of intense emotions threatens to spill tears down my face. I turn, unable to face him, and rush into the small bathroom. With my palm on the door, I shut it soundlessly and collapse onto the edge of the old claw-foot tub.

For years, I've held a grudge against Elijah for taking my virginity and then cheating on me only weeks later. His actions were what finally made me decide to cut ties with the bayou and run as far and fast as I could in the opposite direction, working my ass off to make sure I never had to go back.

And I never knew the truth of why he did it.

My throat burns with the punch of reality.

I've hated him for years when he didn't deserve it. Elijah was a realist. He knew I wasn't a quitter. I wouldn't have quit on him . . . but I might have quit on school if it came down to it. He gutted me, but he did it so I could have the future I desperately wanted.

He's the noble one, and I'm the harpy.

I take several deep breaths, and when my knees no longer feel so shaky, I rise and face the mirror.

My decision from moments ago—go forward and not back—seems more callous now than it did. Nothing is black and white, and apparently nothing is what it seems on the surface. Elijah isn't the cheating asshole I thought he was, all about bagging as many chicks as possible instead of committing to me.

Even this rush of emotion doesn't change the fact that what I felt for him is in the past. But at least I can look back at our past without bitterness and anger now.

He's not for me, but I do owe him an apology, and maybe a thank-you.

I splash cold water on my face, wipe the raccoon circles from under my eyes, and attempt to tame my hair into a ponytail before slipping on the robe I keep on the back of the door.

When I head back into the bedroom, Elijah has his back to me as he pulls a DEVEREUX RECYCLING T-shirt over his head. The taut muscles of his back show scars that weren't there before. Scars I recognize from helping patch Rafe up a few times.

Bullet wounds.

I don't even want to know how he got them, but it's another reminder that going back to the life I left in the bayou means stepping onto the wrong side of the law.

I don't do that anymore.

I'm a successful upstanding citizen.

Granted, my boss is married to the scariest

criminal in the city, but I decide that's not really a relevant factoid.

Because nothing's black and white.

Elijah breaks the silence before I do. "I just texted my guy, and your Bronco hasn't moved. They've kept hands off and haven't chopped it. He also said they don't like having anything sitting intact too long, so we gotta move if we want to get there before they lose patience and it's gone."

"Thank you."

He nods. "No problem."

"Not for that." I shake my head and swallow. "For the other. Everything else. What you did. You—"

"You don't need to thank me. I didn't do anything but show you I wasn't a good bet. That's the truth."

"You believed in me. In my dreams. Didn't run me down for wanting more than the bayou and that little life. You didn't question me or make me explain myself. You just . . . let me be, and then you let me go." My words are rough by the end of my speech.

Elijah drops his gaze to the floor for a beat before meeting mine. "We all want more, Tempe, but you were the only one who had the drive to actually get there. Proud of you."

"Thank you."

He gives me a nod. "Now, you ready to get your Bronco back?"

"Yeah. I am."

He heads for the door. "I'll meet you out front in

my ride."

Before I can respond, he snags his boots and walks out the door.

I'm out front in less than five minutes and find Elijah double-parked in his old Ford truck. *The same truck he . . .* I don't finish my thought.

I reach for the old silver handle, tug it open, and climb inside. "Figured you would've scrapped this thing by now."

"Nah, this truck's vintage. Worth a hell of a lot more whole. But I'll never sell it. At least, not unless shit gets real bad."

As the old truck rolls forward, I ask, "Where we headed?"

"Other side of town. Somewhere you're going to pretend you've never seen and will definitely never talk about ever again." He gives me a sidelong glance at the stop sign. "You catch my drift."

"So I'm the blind, deaf, and dumb girl this morning." I look out the window, taking in the sole man in a suit on his way to work way too early on this Saturday morning. "Got it."

"You know how it goes. It ain't your Bronco. It's one I've been looking for to build out for a friend."

"Mm-hmm," I say, still avoiding looking at Elijah, and that's when I see *him*. I stiffen in my seat, my shoulders going poker straight as I take in the man sitting at a café table with a coffee in front of him.

I blink to make sure I'm not crazy, but . . . *it's him. My stranger from the club.*

Except instead of wearing a suit, he's dressed in a T-shirt and jeans and has a Voodoo Kings hat on his head, shading his eyes—eyes that are looking directly at me.

There's no tint on the windows of Elijah's truck, so there's absolutely nothing to hide that I'm staring at him. Recognition is stamped on his features.

The man in a suit slows as he approaches the café. He pulls a thick newspaper folded in half out from under his arm and drops it on the table in front of my stranger as he walks by, not even missing a beat.

My stranger never looks at the man. Never looks at the newspaper. He's completely focused on me.

Elijah is talking, but his words sound like they're coming from underwater because my head is churning with what I just saw.

Was that a drop?

Who is he?

We pass the café and my stranger's stare burns into me. As though compelled, my head turns to hold his gaze as Elijah's truck continues forward.

"Tempe. Temperance?"

I jerk my attention back to Elijah. "What?"

"You just went catatonic. What the fuck's going on?"

"I don't know. I just . . . thought I saw someone I knew."

He glances in the rearview. "Guys in suits are your type now, I guess. Who would've guessed?"

My curiosity piqued, I spin around and look out the back window to see the man in the suit staring after the truck, even as he walks around the corner.

I don't recognize him at all, but he looks like he's seen me.

A chill washes over me. *What the hell is going on?*

"I was wrong. Never seen him in my life," I say, turning around and directing my attention forward.

"Probably a good thing. Pretty sure that guy works for your boss's husband."

My gaze cuts to Elijah. "What? Which guy?"

"The guy in the suit." Elijah shrugs. "I could be wrong. Might be a different guy. Guess that means you're safe from all that shit-by-association, so it doesn't really matter to you."

Even though my mind is racing, trying to figure out what kind of connection my stranger could possibly have to Lachlan Mount, king of the criminal underworld, I still manage to mumble out a reply. "I stay as far out of it as I can. As in, it doesn't exist for me."

"I wondered why you didn't call him and called me instead."

It's a valid question. "Rafe didn't answer. You were my next thought. It's not like I want to drag my problems to my boss's doorstep when she's just left on vacation."

Elijah turns to look at me before he pulls onto a busier street. "Rafe didn't answer you either? I thought it was just me he wasn't taking calls from right now."

For the second time in a few minutes, chills rack my body. "How many times have you tried to call him?"

"Enough to know that he's really fucking radio silent this time. I figured he'd always answer your calls, no matter what."

Concern for whatever my brother has gotten himself into floods my belly. "I always thought he would too."

CHAPTER 27

Temperance

'M IN MY BRONCO, LIBERATED FROM THE warehouse I'm now going to pretend doesn't exist, driving back to my apartment.

When I roll past the café, I slow down to only a few miles per hour. All the tables are full now, and not a single one of them holds a broad-shouldered man with tattoos and a piercing stare.

It's not like I expected him to still be there, but part of me hoped he would be so I could finally get some answers. Like, what the hell he was doing so close to my apartment? Was he watching me?

When I find a rare open spot in front of my place, I park and climb out of the Bronco, taking care to lock the doors.

I don't know how I got so lucky as to still have my sculpture in the back, untouched, but I did. Probably thanks to Elijah. If not for him, this thing would have been long gone.

It's apparently the day for thanking him repeatedly.

He actually looked pretty uncomfortable when I told him that, at least until he told me he still expected me to deliver on a favor when he needed it, no questions asked. I don't want to know what it's going to be, but it's not like I could have said no.

I head for the gate and unlock it. With the clang of the wrought iron behind me, I take a half-dozen steps and freeze when my gaze locks on the table in the courtyard.

There's a newspaper on it. A newspaper I don't remember seeing there when I left.

I rush to the back door of Harriet's house and knock on the door. *Maybe she came home and I didn't know it?*

I wait, but there's no answer. I bang harder. "Harriet?"

Still no answer.

With my heart somewhere in the vicinity of my throat, I move toward the newspaper. It's splattered with what looks like coffee.

He was here.

In the courtyard.

Oh. My. God.

I flip the paper over, and the headline on the front page sends my stomach plummeting to my feet.

GREGOR STANDISH, CELEBRATED ARTIST, COMMITS SUICIDE

Oh. My. Fucking. God.

My knees turn to water and I collapse into the chair.

Standish is dead. But I am not naive enough to believe the newspaper.

Someone killed him.

I have to talk to Keira. She's the only person who can tell me if I need to freak the fuck out or if I need to calm my overactive imagination. I know what has happened to people who cross Mount, whether knowingly or not, and everything in me says this is another case of *I need to pretend I've never heard of the man before.*

I reach out with trembling fingers and fold the paper closed, but something falls from between the pages.

A black business card. It has the same emblem that was on the other cards the stranger gave me, along with another time and date.

Tonight.

* * *

I can't do this.

Really, I can't do this.

I'm pruning in the bathtub, but I add more hot

water anyway. I can't stop staring at the folded news-paper on the edge of the sink, and the black business card on the glass shelf above the basin.

If I stay in the bathtub, I can avoid reality.

If I get out, I have to decide what I'm going to do tonight.

I want answers, but I don't. I really don't want to think about what connection the stranger may have to Standish's death.

I don't even want to think about the fact that he's dead.

It's all my fault. If I hadn't had an extra sculp-ture in my office, they couldn't have screwed up and brought mine up instead of Standish's. And then he wouldn't have gone off and smeared Seven Sinners on every social media and advertising platform known to man.

But he did. And now he's dead.

I can't believe it.

How am I going to tell Keira? That is, assuming she doesn't already know. She has to know. Right?

Why am I so shocked by this?

Because it's death. Death never becomes mun-dane. It's always shocking. It should be. That's what makes me a normal human being.

So does my guilt.

I spend another fifteen minutes tearing myself up over it before I shut it down. It doesn't matter how long I spend blaming myself. He's dead. Nothing I do or say is going to change that. My guilt isn't going to disappear because I had a hand in his death, even if I didn't order it or pull the trigger.

Because there's no way Standish did it himself.

It's with a million contradictory thoughts crashing together in my head that I drive to Noble Art, hoping against hope that after my car debacle, Valentina still wants this sculpture and maybe a few more.

When I'll have time to create them, I have no idea, but . . . if Valentina says they're marketable and can produce a profit, wouldn't it be wrong not to do it?

In some small way, don't I owe it to Gregor Standish to pursue it? After all, my artwork is part of the reason he's no longer walking this earth, which is ridiculously morbid to consider.

I pull into an open spot across the street from Noble Art and park my car.

I can do this. I will do this.

"Temperance! You got your car back!"

Valentina's voice comes from across the street. This time, she has a baby strapped to her front, and I can't help but smile at how she manages to look stylish with a baby as an accessory. Apparently, that's the fashionable thing these days, at least with this gorgeous couple.

I open the car door and smile genuinely, maybe for the first time all day. "I sure did, *and—*"

"You got the sculpture?" Valentina looks like she's holding her breath.

"I did."

She claps her hands quietly before checking both directions and crossing the street. "Can we see it?"

I gaze down at the dark-haired little guy. "He slept through that? Wow. Of course."

Valentina laughs. "He could sleep through a nuclear blast. This one is a trouper. Which is why I said we should stop at one, but Rix disagrees. We're currently having an argument, and by argument, I mean he's trying to intimidate me into it. I swear, the man doesn't realize his intimidation just makes me want to climb him." She taps her cheek. "Maybe that's his game? I wonder if it's reverse psychology. Tricky bastard. Anyway, let's see it."

I lead her around the back of the Bronco and open the window, lowering the tailgate before pulling the blanket aside.

"It's much easier to appreciate when it's upright, but—"

Valentina interrupts me by holding up a hand. "It's gorgeous. And look at the materials you used for the base—what is that?"

"Part of an empty keg."

Her eyes light up. "I love it so much. Seriously, upcycling is so chic lately, and I get requests all the time for more industrial pieces, especially from all the people rehabbing warehouses into offices and condos." She pulls out her phone and taps in a text. "Rix is going to be swinging by in a bit, so I'll have him bring some help and we'll get it inside. In the meantime, you need to tell me what else you have."

I close up the back of the Bronco, and have a hard time keeping my gaze off it as we cross the street and step into Noble Art.

"I don't have any other completed pieces at the moment available for sale, but it doesn't take me too long."

She studies me. "How would you feel about me commissioning some pieces from you? Making some suggestions. Would that mess with your process? If it does, then we don't have to—"

"No. Actually, I kind of love that idea. I can't promise it'll look exactly like what you're envisioning, but creating something specific is a fun challenge."

"I was really hoping you'd say that." Valentina's smile grows wider. "Because I have a few ideas in my head that I think would be fabulous, and I'd pretty much have them sold before you even finished."

She reaches for a sketch pad and starts drawing a few items, and my excitement climbs with every line she leaves behind on the paper.

A bridge. A skyscraper. The scales of justice.

"I know it seems like a random collection, but I have a few interior designers always hounding me for pieces like this. They'd snap these pieces up faster than you could haul them into the gallery. Do you think you could do it?"

I tap the edge of the paper and look up at her. "Of course."

"Then we have the million-dollar question—how much?"

My brain tells me to go salesman and start high before negotiating to something in the middle, but I decide to take a different tactic with her. "Before the auction, I couldn't imagine that anyone would pay much for one of these, let alone what they did. I know that's because it was a charitable donation, which definitely affects generosity, but . . . I'm totally out of my depth here, Valentina. I need you to give me a starting point so I don't totally screw this up and have you kicking me out the door before we even get the first one in."

Her smile, genuine and brilliant, reveals her straight white teeth. "I appreciate your honesty. How about I put together a proposal for all five pieces— the one you've completed and four others—and then we discuss it?"

"That sounds perfect."

CHAPTER 28

Temperance

"**W**ow." I stare at the sculpture in the center of the gallery in awe.

"Pretty cool, isn't it?"

One of Valentina's employees, an art student named Trinity, stands beside me.

"Amazing."

"I cried the first time she hung one of my paintings on the wall. It was hard to believe that it was *real*."

"I totally get that."

"I mean, to be more accurate, I should probably say it was insane because someone actually *bought it* ten minutes later. For real money."

My smile tugs so hard at my lips, I feel like my face might split. I glance at Trinity. "That's incredible. What a dream come true."

"It was only a real dream because Valentina

taught me it was okay to have it. She pushed me. Wouldn't let me quit. Kept me off the wrong track. Because, of course, there was this guy . . ."

"There's always a guy," I mumble.

A deep bark of laughter comes from the back room, and we both look in that direction.

"Sometimes he's the right guy," Trinity says. "Even when he's disguised as the wrong guy."

My brows droop and I turn to meet her gaze. "What does that mean, Obi Wan?"

"Just that sometimes you don't know what you're working with." Rix's tall frame becomes visible in the doorway. "She didn't. She took a leap of faith, and it turned out to be the best jump of her life."

"You sound like a philosopher, not an artist."

Trinity shrugs. "I've loved and lost. What can I say?"

Valentina and Rix come toward us. "Try not to sound so world weary, Trin. You're too young for that," Valentina says.

"She's too damn young for a lot of things, and she still does them," Rix adds.

"Okay, you two, stop it. Temperance is going to think I'm still an eighteen-year-old idiot."

"You said it, not me." Rix's ribbing comes out with an edge of laughter.

Before the banter can continue, the door chime rings again and a couple comes in.

"I was hoping you could make it. Even quicker

than I expected," Valentina says before moving toward the couple.

But they're not looking at her or paying attention to a word she says. They're moving directly to the center of the room where my sculpture stands.

"It's breathtaking."

The man finally cuts his gaze to Valentina. "How did you know? How are you always right?"

"It's a gift."

The woman reaches out but draws her hand back before it touches the metal.

"It's okay," I tell her. "You can touch it if you want. It's sturdy."

Both of them jerk their chins sideways to face me.

"Is this the artist?" the man asks Valentina, his attention still on me.

When she doesn't answer right away, I realize she's giving me the option of deciding how to play it.

"I'm Temperance . . . and yes. That's my piece." It feels so *amazing* to admit it.

The man rushes toward me and holds out a hand. "I don't know why Valentina hasn't found you before now, but this is *exactly* what we need for the loft. It's perfect. Tell me, what other pieces do you have? I need . . ."

When I walk out of Noble Art with a check in my purse, I may as well be walking on clouds.

Instead of waiting until she had the time to put together a proposal, Valentina launched into negotiations with the couple, starting off with, "Did you know that one of her pieces recently sold for fifty thousand?"

When the couple didn't even blink, Valentina went to town. She got forty thousand for the piece, and less her commission, I now have a check for more money than I make in over half a year.

From my artwork.

Something created out of scrap metal. Based only on the image in my brain and the skills I taught myself.

How crazy is that?

I'm practically bouncing in the seat of my Bronco, unable to contain my excitement. This is *surreal*.

I pull out my phone to call Rafe because he's never going to believe it. When the call goes directly to voice mail, a little of my enthusiasm gives way to fear.

Where are you, Rafe? Are you okay?

Our father left the house one day in a boat and never came back, and my deepest fear, other than failure, is that I'll lose my brother the same way. That he'll leave one day and disappear, leaving me with too many questions and no answers.

He's all I have.

I call back and get his voice mail again, and this

time, with the tremor of threatening tears in my voice, I tell him what I did. How proud I am. How proud I hope he is.

When I hang up, a tear tips over my lower lid. I pray my brother gets to hear my message, and I beg everything that's holy to let me see him tomorrow.

Please don't miss my birthday, Rafe.

⋆⋆━━━ • ━━━⋆⋆

Do I go or don't I?

Of all the thoughts circling in my head, most of them a million times more important, that one keeps bubbling up to the surface.

The business card is on my coffee table, next to the folded coffee-splattered newspaper, and I'm trying to figure out what the two things have in common—besides one mysterious man whose name I don't even know.

Who probably bought my artwork.

Who the hell are you? I pull out my work computer and find the auctioneer's email address, then fire off a quick note as I curse my crap memory. The questions don't slow.

Was he sitting at the café for me? Or was he waiting there for a meeting? Because that's definitely what it looked like.

Does he work for Mount? Or was Elijah completely wrong?

Did he have something to do with Standish's death?

I shut down those questions and pace my apartment with another worry in mind—worry for my brother. Sitting here all night thinking about everything that could have happened to him is going to drive me crazy.

I have two choices to block it out—go to the club or go to Elijah's scrap yard.

Two very different men.

Two very different places.

Two very different motives.

What do I do?

CHAPTER 29

❧⸺•⸺❧

Temperance

F Harriet were home, I would sit in the courtyard with her, drink wine, and listen to stories about her incredible life. But she's not here. She's out living.

With one last glance at the walls that feel like they're closing in on me, I head for my closet and assess my options, like somehow finding the right outfit will dictate what I do tonight. I'm fresh out of little black or red dresses and sexy skirts. My activities of late mean that I've worn every sexy piece of clothing I have, and of course, I haven't had time to do laundry or go to the dry cleaner. Because, I don't know, I've spent way too much time either working or sneaking around and having the best sex of my life.

The best sex of my life.

The thought lights up all the dormant parts of my brain, and suddenly I'm wondering why I'm even second-guessing the idea of going to the club.

Oh, wait, that's right. I don't know who he is and can't risk getting any more attached to a guy whose life is *complicated*.

I could uncomplicate it for him, I think as I flip through the hangers in my closet while berating myself for even considering it.

Work clothes. Work clothes. Old work clothes. Older work clothes.

If I were being judged by the contents of my closet, I'm pretty sure someone could come to only one conclusion. My life is boring.

I've spent so much of my time working and trying to be respectable that I've basically dug myself a cozy little hole in the ground where I'm content to hang out until I'm eventually buried in it.

Great. Let's get morbid.

I head for my dresser and open the top drawer where my limited collection of sexy lingerie lives. It's empty. Because I desperately need to do laundry. Next drawer down. *Yoga pants.* Below that? *Ripped jeans.*

I bet I could go into Harriet's house and find a more exciting wardrobe than I have. But then again, it's not like I've spent any money that I've scrimped and saved on a closet full of clothes that would be suitable for going out and painting the town red. *Or for spending more time at a sex club.*

That settles it then. I'm not going. I will make

my decision by default based on my lack of clothing options.

I reach for the yoga pants and consider pulling them on and making myself at home in my bed with a book. I have enough toy options and batteries in the nightstand drawer to keep myself well satisfied. *I don't need him.*

It's not the same, the devil sitting on my shoulder reminds me, as though I actually need reminding. I don't. I know it's not the same. I know there's nothing like the thrill of walking up those steps and into one of those rooms and letting my instincts take over. That's the problem—my instincts can't be trusted. They led me back there too many times for my own good.

But what if I just went one more time.

One. More. Time.

The words punch through my brain like a chant from a million fans packed into a massive arena.

Screw it. I toss the yoga pants onto my bed and head back into the kitchen to find my phone, which, after girls' night, has a bunch of new numbers.

Do I feel good about asking one of them for help this early in the possible friendship? Not really, but I'm desperate.

I pull up Yve Titan's contact and tap to open a new message.

TEMPERANCE: *Is your lingerie store open tonight?*

Her reply comes as soon as I make it back to my bedroom.

YVE: *I'm here right now. You need something?*
TEMPERANCE: *You work Saturday nights?*
YVE: *Man's out of town. Might as well make bank. Come spend some money. I'll hook you up with some goodies.*
TEMPERANCE: *On my way.*

Yve replies with an emoji of a woman in a red dress.

I guess I could wear red again tonight . . .

<hr />

Pretty Kitty, which is located right next to Dirty Dog, has the cutest magenta storefront that I've never noticed before.

Yve greets me with a smile and a quick hug as soon as I step inside. "You made it!"

"I'm probably making a terrible decision."

Her eyes widen. "Those are usually the best kind. You want to tell me about it?"

"Remember when I mentioned that club?"

She chokes on a laugh. "Like I could forget? I'm ready to send you back loaded down with business cards so I can get some more traffic through my doors."

"And here I was going to ask you to tell me not to go back."

Her brows dive together. "Now, why in the world would I do that?"

"Because, I . . . I shouldn't be showing up for some booty call with a guy whose name I don't know. It doesn't make any sense. Lord, I shouldn't even be telling you this. You're going to think I'm a whore, and I've only met you once."

"First," she says as she crosses her arms over her adorable teal dress, "I don't go around slut-shaming anyone. You can do whatever you want with whoever you want, and the only way I'd judge you for it—and by judge, I mean *murder you*—is if you came sniffing around my man. Or any of my girls' men. We clear on that?"

All I can manage is a jerky nod. "Of course."

"Good. Then let's talk about the rest of your asinine statement next."

"Asinine? Really?"

"You did say I was going to think you're a whore, did you not?"

Again, my response is a nod.

"What do you have against booty calls?"

"It just seems so . . . impersonal. Doesn't it?"

"You looking to marry this guy?"

I rear back. "Lord, no."

"Then why does it have to be personal? You're a single woman, old enough to think for herself. Why do you feel like you need to justify this to anyone? You want to get laid, go get laid. You don't need to be thinking about china patterns when you do it."

She's right, but I've still got hang-ups. "I don't even know his name."

"Then why don't you call Ari and have her work her little hacker-girl magic and find it? Then you can surprise the shit out of him when you scream it when you come."

After what I saw today, I'm even more curious who the hell my stranger is.

Yve clearly doesn't need me to reply, because she's already decided what path I'm taking tonight.

"Call Ari right now and have her come meet you here. Tell her I've got something that'll blow Hennessy's mind, but she's gotta bring her computer with her and come without him. I'm picking out some drop-dead sexy lingerie for you in the meantime."

Yve sweeps off and heads for a rack of gorgeous bras and underwear.

"I was thinking red."

She spins and shoots me a gorgeous smile. "Of course you were, girl. I got you."

I pull up my emails and look to see if the auctioneer has responded.

Bingo. He has.

Nunya Holdings. It sounds exotic. Maybe he's in some kind of international business?

Yeah, because that's surely what kind of business leads to the weird handoff I saw this morning.

Yve's right; it's time to get some answers. I swipe through my contacts to find Ariel, and I hit CALL.

"Please tell me you have that company name," Ariel says. "I've been dying to start digging so we can figure out who your mystery man is. It literally kept me up last night, which actually resulted in three rounds of . . . never mind. You got a name?" She barely breathes from the moment she answers the phone because she's so busy talking.

"Yes. Yes, I do. Nunya Holdings."

She bursts out laughing. "Nunya? Like *none of your business*?"

"What? You've heard of it?"

Her laughter intensifies. "Dude. Wow. Okay, let's back up. Have you ever asked a question someone didn't want to answer?"

"Of course," I reply, but I'm not following where her logic is headed. Maybe because she's a genius and I'm definitely not?

"Has anyone ever replied *nunya*? As in *none of your business*?"

The pieces click together, and I don't know how I didn't see it before. "Are you telling me that company name is a joke?"

Her laughter cuts off. "I'd say it was named by someone who has an interesting sense of humor."

"Tell her to come down. I've got goodies for her,"

Yve says as she returns to my side, carrying a few different sets of red lingerie.

"Was that Yve?" Ariel asks.

"I'm at Pretty Kitty. She wants you to come down."

"And bring your computer," Yve adds.

"I don't know why you didn't lead with that. I'll be on my way in ten. Be warned, I'm on day-four hair. It's ninety percent dry shampoo at this point, and I'm not even going to apologize for it."

Ariel is certainly one of a kind, I think as I say, "Got it."

When I hang up, Yve holds up her handfuls of hangers. "Let's get you in the fitting room. I can't wait to see you in these so you can blow this guy's mind."

I follow her to one of the pale pink doors in the back of the shop that surround a cute little boudoir area, and wait outside while she hangs up her selections.

"If something doesn't fit, let me know. Holler when you're ready."

When I step into the dressing room, my mind is only half on the lingerie, and the other half is firmly on the ridiculous company name.

None of your business. Really?

Does that mean my stranger is a con man, or he just has a sense of humor?

As I slip on a gorgeous red lace bra that reveals more than it conceals, I can't figure out an answer.

When Ariel arrives, I'm just slipping back into my street clothes and have selected my armor for tonight.

"Rhett tried to come with, until I told him that I wouldn't buy anything unless it was going to be a surprise, and then he conceded. I swear, even the strongest man can be brought low with the right lingerie."

Yve gives her a quick hug. "Damn right. Now, did you bring that fancy computer of yours along with your big brain so we can figure out Temperance's mystery?"

Ariel raises her arm and points to her large purse. "I barely leave home without it. But first, tell me you have something in lavender. I don't know why I'm obsessed with that idea, but I have a feeling it's a good one."

"I'll give you lavender as soon as you figure out who Mr. Sex Club is."

"I see. That's my carrot." Ariel glances around. "Now, where are the whips?"

Yve winks. "In the back corner. Get to work."

Ariel blushes. "On it."

She leaves Yve and me behind to make herself at home on the stool behind the checkout counter. As soon as she has a laptop in front of her, it's like watching her morph into a different person.

"You sweep this place for bugs? I'm assuming Titan would, but we can never be too careful."

Yve's brow arches. "Just do your thing and let me

worry about this place."

"You wouldn't be so cavalier if you were the one risking federal prison to find this stuff."

"Oh my God," I blurt out. "Are you serious? If that's the case, then don't—"

Ariel cracks her knuckles with a grin. "Don't worry. I'm not going to get caught."

Then she goes to work. It takes her less than sixty seconds to start spouting off information.

"Nunya Holdings is a domestic corporation, but the only shareholder listed is another company."

"It's a front?"

She shrugs without looking up. "Not necessarily. It could be part of an overall entity structure. I have plenty of companies that only have another company as a member."

It's so strange to think that this little redhead-ed spitfire is the CEO of a huge conglomeration of companies.

"Did you know I'm a billionaire today? Bitcoin for the win!" Ariel says, totally offhand, and goes back to typing.

Yve looks from Ariel to me and laughs. "That girl is nuts."

I'm not sure if I should agree with her or not.

Within minutes, Ariel is three layers deep into the corporate structure when creases appear between her swooped eyebrows. "They're actually really damn good at this stuff. Everything goes back to a generic registered-agent company and their database is en-crypted, so it'll take me a bit longer to find some an-swers there."

"So you can't—"

"Never say can't. I just need to look somewhere else. Somewhere you don't need to know exists."

Yve's arms are crossed over her chest again. "You're doing that dark-web shit, aren't you?"

Ariel looks up with a scowl. "Shhh. No need to invite bad mojo by talking about the thing we don't speak about."

My gaze ping-pongs back and forth between them as they talk about the dark web, which, inci-dentally, I actually thought was some fake thing they only talk about in movies. Apparently, I'm more shel-tered than I thought, because it's real.

"Dark web is harder to trace. There are a lot of bad people with great skill sets that make it really hard for anyone to find anything, let alone find the thing they're actually looking for. But you're in luck, because I'm better than all of them."

Ariel's confidence is somehow comforting, and Yve pulls light purple lingerie from her racks as Ariel keeps working.

"This is weird," the hacker murmurs.

"What's weird?" I take a step closer, attempting to look at her over the screen covering her face.

"The structure of companies doesn't bring up *anything* on the dark web."

"Why is that weird?" My question is genuine because I feel truly naive about this stuff.

"Because even normal companies usually have their company information available for sale by someone who stole it. Nunya and its family of companies are a dead end."

"So, what does that mean?"

Ariel finally looks up and meets my gaze. "Someone works really hard or pays a lot of money for these companies not to exist on the dark web."

"So?"

"So, that's something most companies would never even think about doing. Which means . . ."

"What?" My anticipation is skyrocketing.

"It means that whoever runs those companies is actively working on keeping them off here. Invisible. That's not normal, by the way. Most people don't even know how to access the dark web. But these people are not only on it, they're experts."

A feeling of unease creeps over me. "So you're saying he's a criminal?"

She shrugs. "I have no idea, but he definitely knows someone who has skills or the insight to tell him to do this."

She types furiously on the keyboard while I try to decide what to make of that information.

"Wait, wait a minute. I found something. Whoa. Real-time shit. Hold on to your panties, girls." Her fingers fly.

"What?"

"I've got a payment trail that leads from someone who's sloppy. Well, sloppier than your guy. A bank in Mauritius just transferred money to one of the shell companies linked to Nunya. It just happened, which means Nunya hasn't had time to erase the evidence yet."

"Where the hell is Mauritius?" Yve asks before I can voice the question.

"Island off the coast of Madagascar. It's a tax haven. Lots of companies are incorporated there for tax and privacy purposes. This payment just happened. Wow. Whatever this company does, they must do it well, because they just got five hundred grand."

"A half-million dollars? For what?"

Ariel shakes her head. "No way to know, but generally, you see the biggest payments for drugs, hits, information, and human trafficking."

"Okay, those all sound really bad."

Ariel keeps typing at lightning speed. "Of course they're bad. Otherwise, they'd be using PayPal. Whoa, yep. There it goes. If I hadn't been on here and digging, I never would've seen it. Holy shit. I think they know I found it."

Her fingers burst into even faster action. "Fuck. They've might've found me. I gotta wrap this up. Shit. Not good."

Yve and I share a concerned look. "Shut it down!"

Ari shakes her head. "Can't. Gotta cover my tracks."

I've never seen anyone work as quickly or in a more focused fashion than Ariel does in the next few minutes.

"Suck on that, dickhole." She sounds triumphant when she closes her laptop with a decisive click.

"What just happened?" I ask her.

"You asked for help . . . I helped. And now the trails are cleared and they can't trace my searches back to me."

"Are you sure?"

She flips her hair and rolls her eyes. "Didn't I mention that I'm the best?"

Yve giggles. "If you don't remember, she'll tell you again. I swear, I've never met anyone more impressed with her own computer skills than this one."

"It's well deserved. It's not like I'm bragging. I'm just that good. Now, where's my lavender lingerie? I've got a man to seduce. He doesn't know I'm a billionaire yet. Hopefully, he doesn't mind."

CHAPTER 30

Temperance

W HEN I PULL UP AT THE CLUB, I'M MORE
certain than ever that I'm making the right
decision, if only for one reason—I need
answers.

Who the hell he is. What he does. Why he was
in my neighborhood. If and how he's connected to
Mount. If he truly bought my artwork, and what he
did with it.

Finally, I want to know if I have to decide to never
see him again because he's involved with something
awful and horrible, and my life isn't going down the
criminal path. Except, of course, guilt by association
with my boss and her husband . . . and whatever the
hell my brother is doing.

Nothing's black and white.

With my mask tied on and a vintage black dress
from Dirty Dog covering my new hot-red bra and

panties, I climb up the stairs behind the masked man to whom I gave my card. He hands it back to me as soon as he opens the front door for me.

Tonight, it's louder inside. More chatter is coming from upstairs, like the guests aren't afraid of being overheard. That's new and different.

What isn't new and different? The fact that Magnolia is just inside the foyer and her eyes lock on me.

"I wondered if you'd show tonight. He didn't think you would."

There's no question about who *he* is.

"Where is he?" I ask.

Something flashes over her face before I can read it. "Come on up with me."

Magnolia leads me up to the second floor, to the door where the light spills out from underneath along with the strains of jazz. The only time I've been inside that room is when she took me on a tour, but I know it's the public area of the club.

As soon as she opens the door and my gaze sweeps the room, I know he's not here.

"Is he late?"

Magnolia leads me to the bar. "You need a drink, I think. You look like you've had a long day."

I reach out to put a hand on her arm. "Don't bullshit me, Mags. Is he late or not coming?"

"What makes you think he's not coming?"

"I just need a straight answer. If he's not here,

then I wasted my trip and I have the answer I needed—that I should've followed my first instincts and never come back."

"Don't be so hasty now, girl. Maybe there are forces at work here that you can't understand." When she glances over her shoulder, I pin her gaze with my own.

"Is he here or not?"

She shakes her head. "No. He's not. Something came up. He called and asked if I'd give you his regrets. He'll be in touch."

What could have come up? Is he okay? Did something happen with the guy at the café? Did it have something to do with the five hundred grand someone paid him that Ariel tracked on the dark web?

A dozen possibilities pop into my brain, and I have no idea what's right or wrong. None of them are good possibilities.

"I have to go," I tell Magnolia. "This was a mistake."

I turn on my heel and head for the door. However, instead of executing a graceful exit, I run smack into the chest of a man—and it's not the man I want to see. It's another stranger, and this one I don't care to know.

"Who is this delightful little creature, Magnolia? And where have you been hiding her? You afraid of some competition?" His voice is smooth and cultured, and immediately puts me on edge with its smug, condescending tone.

"She's just leaving," Magnolia tells him, her voice coming from right behind me.

"Not until I get a chance to talk with her."

"So sorry, sir. She's intent on leaving, so I'd appreciate it if you wouldn't stand in her way."

He holds out his hand to me, completely ignoring Magnolia. "It's a pleasure to make your acquaintance . . ." He pauses, clearly expecting me to give him my name, but this isn't my first time here and I'm not about to offer it.

"I have to go."

I take another step but his hand closes around my arm, just above my elbow.

"But the night is young, and I've been out of town for months. Who knows when I'll have a chance to get back here. My work so often keeps me away." His gaze drifts back to Magnolia. "Much to my regret."

Magnolia's eyes narrow on him. "Giles, let her go."

"Sorry, *sir*," I tell him. "I'm not a member. Good luck with the rest of your night."

I really want to tell him that actin g so overbearing makes me assume he has a tiny dick, but I don't. Maybe it's his overbearing nature that makes Magnolia look like she wants to slice and dice him, but I truly have no idea. The guy could just be another person out looking for a thrill, like me. But then again, he wouldn't carry the creeper vibe so strongly if he wasn't one. For the first time, I truly feel uncomfortable in a way that makes me feel unsafe here.

This is why Rafe told me not to come here. I should have listened to my brother.

When I tug free of Giles, I hurry out of the room, leaving Magnolia behind to do damage control. Maybe it's rude, but I don't know him and she does.

That's when it occurs to me—*she said his name.*

I pause at the top step, taking in the shiny wooden banister that leads down the stairs to the front door. The front door I've run out like the devil was on my heels once before.

I'm tempted to do it again right now, but instead, I walk out calmly.

I shouldn't care that I finally decided to come and he's not here, but some creepy guy was and Magnolia broke the rules. I shouldn't care that I don't have any way to track down my stranger to get my answers to a hell of a lot of questions I have.

I shouldn't care about any of it . . .

But I do.

CHAPTER 31

Temperance

THE BLINDINGLY BRIGHT SUNLIGHT CUTS through my curtains, waking me up from a restless night.

It's my birthday.

Others might wake to a phone call from a parent, but not me. Not this year. And really, not ever.

Rafe has always been the best big brother he could manage to be, given his unconventional lifestyle, but even that can't make up for having parents who don't give a damn about you.

I push all that heartache-inducing crap out of my head and roll out of bed.

I only get one first day of my next trip around the sun, and I may as well begin it as I mean to go on—by kicking ass and taking names.

It's Sunday, and barring any emergencies at the distillery, I've got the whole day to myself before I meet Rafe for dinner.

If he shows up for dinner. The possibility that he won't show is twisting my guts into knots, which isn't helping set the tone for an optimistic day.

He. Will. Be. There.

I repeat it like a mantra as I head for the bathroom to splash some water on my face and get ready.

Mission one for my birthday is to get a head start on creating another piece for Valentina. I have my marching orders and a little bit of free time, so I may as well get started on chasing this dream for real.

As soon as I'm dressed in old jeans and a faded Springsteen T-shirt, I grab my phone and my purse and shove my feet into a tattered pair of black Chucks by the front door.

Fifteen minutes later, I have a cup of coffee, a beignet, and some Springsteen on the radio as I head for the bayou. Does it seem a little strange that my path forward is taking me on a detour through my past? I lick powdered sugar off my fingertips as I consider it.

Maybe it's cathartic. Or something. I don't know.

When I pull up in front of the closed metal gate, I honk my horn and wait.

Elijah's truck sits in front of the trailer he lives in, just behind the barbed wire. Another car sits out front too. I don't recognize it, but it doesn't take a genius to figure out that Elijah isn't pining for me all that hard. In some way, that assures me that I made the right decision.

I honk again, getting some kind of perverse satisfaction out of the fact I might be interrupting his sleep or his morning quickie. He pokes his head out the front door.

"The hell are you doing here so early?" he yells.

"Need to work. Dogs loose?"

"Yeah. Hold on." He steps out, sweatpants hanging low on his hips, and shoves two fingers in his mouth to produce a sharp whistle. The two Cane Corsos come running out from between the shells of cars.

They bound up the stairs to the trailer, and Elijah leads them to their kennel beside it before coming toward me.

I wait until he reaches the gate before I speak. "Sorry if I'm interrupting your morning."

He gives me a pointed look. "You ain't sorry."

"And you weren't really missing me that much."

He hauls the metal gate open. "Best way to get over someone is to get under someone else."

I drive through the gate and he shuts it behind me. "Thanks, Eli. Appreciate it."

"Happy birthday, Tempe. I'll swing in and check on you . . . later."

Before I can respond, a brassy blonde sticks her head out of the front door of the trailer.

"Eli, bed's getting cold, and so is your chance at a second round this morning."

I don't recognize her, and that's plenty fine with me.

"You better get back to it."

He grins and salutes me.

For some dumb reason, I'm feeling more alone than ever when I drive up to the big metal building and park.

Best thing I can do? Channel that emotion into my art. A torch always has a way of making me feel better.

⸻ · ⸻

Six hours later, my body is sore from dismantling, hauling, hammering, and welding, but I have another piece halfway finished.

"What's that one going to be?" Elijah asks from the door.

I turn and flip up my welding mask. "A skyline."

"Damn, that's gonna be sweet. Big too. You gonna sell it in that fancy gallery?"

"That's the plan."

"Guess that means you're gonna need a steady supply of new and interesting metal to keep up with demand."

"Probably."

"If you want to put out some cash, I can throw up an ad for scrap metal by the pound. Hundred bucks max per person. Might get you some interesting stuff.

People around here could really use the money."

It's a smart idea, I decide, as I consider it. "I can lay out a grand for it, but nothing more than that right now."

"I'll set it up."

I lean against the workbench. "Why are you helping me? I thought you'd start off with charging me some crazy rent to keep using this space. Wasn't that your plan?"

He shrugs. "Maybe I decided having you come back around is payment enough for now."

"Bullshit."

"You're still gonna help me chop cars if I need it."

I groan. "I knew there was a catch."

"What? You're quick with a grinder, and sometimes I gotta move fast. You happen to be here, you throw in an extra pair of hands so we can get through it."

"And if you get raided? You think I'm going down for it?"

Another shrug. "I ain't gettin' caught."

"So you say."

"So I know. I got people who'll tip me off if things get hot."

"I sure hope so." I tug my gloves off finger by finger and toss them on the workbench before raising the subject that's been eating at me all day. "You heard from Rafe?"

Elijah shakes his head. "Nope. Not at all. Thought

you and him had a date tonight like you always do on your birthday."

It doesn't surprise me that Elijah knows about our long-standing tradition. "He's MIA still. If he doesn't show tonight, I don't know what I'll do."

He grunts. "Seriously? You're working for the man that everyone is terrified of, and you don't know what to do if your brother doesn't show?"

"I work for his wife."

Elijah rolls his eyes. "Same difference. If I were you, if Rafe doesn't show, I'd call in the cavalry, because you know that means shit is bad."

"Thanks for the tip."

"Anytime you want more than the tip . . ."

I flip my helmet down and turn my back on him. "Save it for someone who'll give you a shot."

CHAPTER 32

Temperance

I CHECK MY WATCH AGAIN FOR THE FIFTIETH TIME. I don't know why, because it's not going to change a damn thing.

Rafe isn't here. He's an hour late. His phone goes directly to voice mail every single time I call. My texts have gone unanswered, and the knot in my stomach is roughly the size of my head.

The waitress stops by the table, refilling my water glass for the sixth time. "Would you like to go ahead and order?"

"No, I think I'll give up and go home. I'll take my tab." I gesture to the half glass of room-temperature champagne that sits in front of me.

"Oh, honey, that's on the house. So sorry about your birthday." She looks at me with pity as I reach for my purse.

It's time.

I have to call Keira.

Rafe told me if I felt like something was wrong, I should call Mount.

My brother hasn't missed my birthday in a decade without a damn good reason, and definitely not with this kind of radio silence. Still, calling Keira feels like I'm admitting he may already be beyond help.

I unlock my phone and scroll through the contacts. Before I can tap on Keira's, my screen lights up with a call from her.

Surprised, I answer it immediately. "Hello?"

"Temperance." It's Mount, not my boss, and the sound of his deep voice sends my stomach tumbling.

"How bad is it? Is he dead?" I'm proud of myself for keeping my tone devoid of emotion.

"Ransom? No. Not that I know of."

"Thank God," I whisper.

"But if the people he fucked over get their hands on him, he's going to wish he was in very short order. And they're going to come for you too."

I close my eyes and a sinking sensation overwhelms me. "What do I do?"

"Go home. Right now. Don't stop anywhere. Don't talk to anyone. I'm sending someone to you. He's not the right man for the job, but he's the best I've got, and I trust him more than I trust most anyone. Do what he says. Don't argue."

"Who? How? When?"

"Temperance?" he asks.

"Yes?"

"Stop asking questions. The less you know, the better. He'll be at your place, get you somewhere safe, and keep you from being used as leverage to draw out your brother. That's all you can do right now. If they get you, Ransom is fucked and you're both dead, except it won't be pretty or quick. Don't talk to anyone, especially not your new cop friends."

I'm not sure why I'm shocked Mount knows about my new friendships, but I am. "How do you know—"

"Do you really care right now?"

I shake my head, even though he can't see it. "No. I'm going."

"Good. Be smart."

I barely remember rushing out of the restaurant, because everything blurs together in a smear of fear and terrible possibilities.

"If they get to you, Ransom is fucked and you're both dead."

Mount's words repeat through my brain, and shivers rip down my spine.

Lord help us both.

CHAPTER 33

DON'T COME WHEN I'M CALLED. I'M NOT ANYONE'S fucking dog. But this time . . . I'm making an exception.

The iron gate out by the street clangs shut as I wait silently in Temperance Ransom's apartment. The treads of the spiral staircase creak, signaling her ascent. A few seconds later, her keys jangle and she unlocks the door. When she pushes it open, I step out of the shadows of her miniature living room.

Temperance's entire body tenses when she sees me, her big brown eyes going wide with shock and fear as her purse lands on the floor beside her with a thump.

I don't like that panicked look on her face, especially not when it's aimed in my direction.

"What the hell are you doing here?" Her husky voice punches me in the gut, just like it does every time she speaks.

I shouldn't have touched her that first time at the club . . . or the second . . . or the third, but how the hell was I supposed to stop myself?

She stares at me, barely blinking, waiting for me to answer.

Small talk isn't exactly a skill you acquire in my line of work, so I keep it simple. "I heard you need help."

"He sent *you*? Why? What the hell is going on?"

All fair questions, but none I can answer for her right now. "We gotta move. Come on."

I take a step toward her, and Temperance shrinks back. As much as the move cuts me, I can't fault her instincts for not trusting me.

She shouldn't. It'll keep her alive longer.

"Who are you?" she whispers.

That's one question I have to answer, even though she's not going to want to hear it.

"I'm the man who just took out a half-million-dollar contract to kill your brother."

The Savage Trilogy continues in *Iron Princess*.

ALSO BY MEGHAN MARCH

Take Me Back

Bad Judgment

MOUNT TRILOGY:
Ruthless King
Defiant Queen
Sinful Empire

BENEATH Series:
Beneath This Mask
Beneath This Ink
Beneath These Chains
Beneath These Scars
Beneath These Shadows
Beneath These Lies
Beneath the Truth

FLASH BANG Series:
Flash Bang
Hard Charger

AUTHOR'S NOTE

UNAPOLOGETICALLY SEXY ROMANCE

I'd love to hear from you. Connect with me at:

Website:
www.meghanmarch.com

Facebook:
www.facebook.com/MeghanMarchAuthor

Twitter:
www.twitter.com/meghan_march

Instagram:
www.instagram.com/meghanmarch

ABOUT THE AUTHOR

Meghan March has been known to wear camo face paint and tromp around in the woods wearing mud-covered boots, all while sporting a perfect manicure. She's also impulsive, easily entertained, and absolutely unapologetic about the fact that she loves to read and write smut.

Her past lives include slinging auto parts, selling lingerie, making custom jewelry, and practicing corporate law. Writing books about dirty-talking alpha males and the strong, sassy women who bring them to their knees is by far the most fabulous job she's ever had.

She loves hearing from her readers at
meghanmarchbooks@gmail.com.

CPSIA information can be obtained
at www.ICGtesting.com
Printed in the USA
BVHW030906240319
543532BV00001B/61/P

9 781943 796151